I0822637

The Torso At Highgate Cemetery and other Sherlock Holmes Stories

By Tim Symonds

Hardback: 978-1-80424-290-2
ePub: 978-1-80424-129-5
PDF: 978-1-80424-130-1

Published in the UK by MX Publishing
335 Princess Park Manor, Royal Drive, London, N11 3GX
www.mxpublishing.com

Edited by David Marcum

Cover by Brian Belanger zhahadun@myfairpoint.net

Tim Symonds was born in London. He grew up in Somerset, Dorset and the British Crown Dependency of Guernsey. After several years farming on the slopes of Mt. Kenya and working on the Zambezi River in Central Africa, he emigrated to the United States. He studied at the University of California, Los Angeles, graduating Phi Beta Kappa, and at Göttingen University, in Germany. He is a Fellow of the Royal Geographical Society. Detective novels by the author include - *Sherlock Holmes And The Mystery Of Einstein's Daughter*, *Sherlock Holmes And The Case Of The Bulgarian Codex, Sherlock Holmes And The Dead Boer At Scotney Castle, Sherlock Holmes And The Sword Of Osman, Sherlock Holmes And The Nine-Dragon Sigil, Sherlock Holmes And The Strange Death of Brigadier-General Delves.*

Website http://tim-symonds.co.uk/

To my ever-beautiful partner-in-crime Lesley Abdela

Contents

The Torso at Highgate Cemetery

Part I – Inspector Lestrade Comes Hurrying to 221B, Baker Street

My notes date back to April 1895. The nation would soon be wilting under a heat wave. It wasn't the blistering heat or the fetid smells on the streets outside the lodgings I shared with Sherlock Holmes which I remember most. It was the utter horror I was shortly to experience in a London cemetery.

I had sold my medical practice and settled back at 221B, Baker Street, a London boulevard of brick houses of great respectability and convenience, being close to rail and omnibus routes. When I could get Holmes to sit down, I had an open notebook ever at the ready, checking details of past cases in hopes of publication in *The Strand Magazine* on which my income and Holmes's considerable reputation rested. In particular I wanted to commit to paper the more obscure features of Holmes's epic struggle four years earlier with the late Professor Moriarty, "The Napoleon of Crime", the most dangerous malefactor Holmes ever encountered.

By 1891 Moriarty's vast criminal enterprise had been so badly affected by Holmes's "predations" that he pursued Holmes and me to the tiny hamlet of Meiringen in the Swiss Alps, where I had reason to believe both had plummeted into the nearby Reichenbach Falls, locked in a violent death-struggle. Unbeknownst to me, Holmes had used his knowledge of *baritsu* to free himself and hurl Moriarty off the cliff edge to his doom.

It was almost three years before Holmes felt safe enough to return to these shores and take his chances with the bitter remnants of the evil Professor's gang, not least former chief-of-staff Colonel Sebastian Moran. The Colonel was the only person who knew Holmes had survived the struggle at the Falls. Where Moran himself was hiding out, biding his time, was the subject of much conjecture.

Now, nearly four years after Holmes's supposed death, my great friend got up and left the breakfast table with "Don't wait up for me tonight, Watson. I shall probably not be back before the witching hour. Your questions have inspired me to make a nostalgic visit to the scene of several of our cases, starting at the barge-building yards of Limehouse and the dark waste of water beyond. Once again, I shall breathe in the fumes of the rum and the stink of stale fish. I shall rub shoulders with boatswains from Canton, cooks from Hainan Island, stevedores and winchmen, yardmasters and boilersmiths."

On the morrow I came down to the breakfast table with a copy of the halfpenny newspaper *The Echo*. It contained an article titled *Daring Robbery. Burglars Break into Scotland*

Yard's Black Museum. Our housekeeper Mrs. Hudson came up the stairs, bringing me a fine breakfast in the Scotch style - broiled kippers, kedgeree, kidneys, scrambled eggs, toast, accompanied by the familiar well-polished, silver-plated coffee pot. I unrolled the napkin and turned to look through the window. The sun had risen to produce a cyan sky dotted with cotton-like cumulus clouds. Inspired by a recent gift of Seebohm's *A History of British Birds*, I would take my customary morning stroll to the nearby Regent's Park to observe the antics of our spring visitors, especially looking out for the garganey, shoveler, wigeon, and pintail.

I poured myself a cup of coffee and picked up *The Echo*. The article titled *Daring Robbery* continued -

> *Only now revealed by Inspector Lestrade of Scotland Yard, a fortnight ago one or more area-sneaks made a daring entry into the Black Museum, the home of criminal memorabilia kept at the headquarters of the Metropolitan Police Service. The Police are still assessing which objects have been stolen. The collection includes letters ascribed to Jack the Ripper and a substantial collection of mêlée weapons, some overt, some concealed, including shotguns disguised as umbrellas, and numerous walking-stick swords, all of which have been used in murders or serious assaults in London.*

I was well-acquainted with the Black Museum. The collection had come into existence over twenty years before as an aid to the police in the study of crime and criminals, a teaching collection for police recruits, and only ever accessible by those involved in legal matters, or Royals and other important persons.

The article ended with '*Despite a blanket of secrecy on the matter,* The Echo *believes one important display may have been a principal target of the thieves, a powerful air-gun, noiseless and of tremendous power.'*

I put the newspaper open at the page on Holmes's chair and turned to an article in *The British Medical Journal* titled *Cholera and The Meccan Pilgrimage*. Outbreaks of the deadly disease were occurring at Kamaran and Djeddah in the Red Sea, and at Mecca itself, blamed on the large number of Mohammedans arriving from Hyderabad. In my time as an Army Assistant Surgeon on the North-West Frontier, I learned no more likely way exists for spreading the deadly bacterium *Vibrio cholerae* to all four corners of the Earth than to have tens of thousands of human-beings setting off for Mecca on the mandatory Haj pilgrimage, sharing make-shift latrines and washing facilities en route.

The clink of horses' hoofs closing in on the pavement came through the open window, followed by the sound of carriage wheels grating heavily against the kerb. I went to the window to catch sight of Scotland Yard Inspector Lestrade leaping from a brougham and striding to our front door. His familiar voice was raised to a high pitch, shouting ahead to our housekeeper.

I raised the window and called down.

"Inspector, if it's Holmes you want, I'm sorry to disappoint you – either he's still asleep or he didn't return last night from a visit to the Docks."

"No matter, Dr. Watson," Lestrade called up, "it's you I've come for! I must ask you to come down at once and accompany me. A body has been found at Highgate Cemetery."

"A body?" I repeated, smiling quizzically. "Is it so surprising, given it's a cemetery?"

"Apparently, it's legless. The first thing we'll want is your estimate of how long he's been dead," Lestrade explained.

He waved a hand around him at the inquisitive gaggle of passers-by already drawing a circle around him.

"I'll tell you more when we're on our way," he added. "At least what little I know at the moment."

I seized my coat and bowler and went down the stairs two at a time. Lestrade said, "Get in the cab, Doctor, and we shall be on our way."

I informed Mrs. Hudson where I was going. The moment I was settled at his side, Lestrade shouted out, "Constable! Highgate Cemetery, if you will! Right. Now, Doctor," he continued, "I can only tell you what I know. A man walking his dog through the graveyard only an hour ago says he came across the torso of a man seated upright on a grave, I say seated, balanced more like because the legs have been chopped off. A ghastly sight, he said. He had to restrain his dog from attacking it. Who has done this – and why – is up to us to determine. The local police have ringed the spot off and forbidden anyone to approach the body."

Lestrade had no other information to provide – simply that my presence had been requested. Twenty minutes of pensive silence ensued until my companion leaned out of the window and shouted, "Constable, can't you go any faster!"

Back came "Only if you and the other gentleman get out and walk, sir. The horses are pulling us up a 426-foot hill, one of the longest and steepest in the whole of London."

The horses' breath became harsher and excessively rapid. I recalled similar signs of respiratory stress from a fine cavalry horse I saved hard to buy during my time on India's boiling North-West Frontier. In the middle of a small but brutal skirmish against the Pathans, I was unable either to stop to rest him or to throw water over him. In the unbearable heat the blood supply to the animal's intestines and kidneys shut down. He dropped dead from under me. I threw open the window and shouted to the driver to bring the brougham to an immediate halt. Lestrade and I clambered out. The driver called down, “Inspector, the entrance is a hundred yards ahead, on your right, sir. You’ll be met by Constable Choat. He’ll tell you where to go.”

Part II – I enter the Cemetery with Lestrade

Highgate cemetery was becoming a fashionable place to enter the Afterlife. Over the years I had attended burials of a number of my more well-to-do patients. A romantic attitude to death and its presentation led to the creation of a labyrinth of Egyptian sepulchres, Gothic tombs, and a litany of silent stone angels, safe from the weathering of cemeteries lower down, a pitting brought about by the Capital’s acute atmospheric pollution. The wild and disused northwestern part of the cemetery was full of mature trees, shrubbery, and wildflowers, providing a haven for birds and small animals.

Constable Choat was blocking off the path to visitors. He saluted, giving me a nod of recognition.

“You’re wanted in the northwestern area, Doctor,” Choat advised, “the heavily overgrown part. A roundabout route via the Circle of Lebanon is the easiest way to get there.”

We soon came upon the Circle. At its heart was a massive cedar tree which must have long predated the cemetery. It towered over the landscape like a huge bonsai, its base surrounded by a circle of tombs.

On spotting our approach, another policeman emerged from the shadow cast by the Circle. Lestrade introduced me. This time, other than a hasty salute the man paid me no attention. He pointed Lestrade towards a patchwork of toppled gravestones and decaying mausolea.

“Over there, Inspector,” he instructed. “Best is if you…”

On saying this, his words came to an abrupt halt. He turned to look at me and then back at Lestrade.

"Inspector," he began, "you said this is Dr. Watson. Do you mean Dr. John H. Watson, the biog – ?"

"The biographer of Sherlock Holmes," I interrupted, smiling. "I am, yes."

The smile was not reciprocated. A look of concern passed across the constable's face. He continued to address Lestrade, saying, "Can we speak over here, sir?"

He moved a short distance away, followed by the Scotland Yard Inspector. I watched as the policeman took out a notebook and read from an open page. He spoke in a whisper. Lestrade's face turned ashen. He turned towards me, looking grim.

"Dr. Watson," he began, "there's something the constable has just told me. It's about the legless corpse we've come to inspect."

"What about it?" I asked.

"I wonder if the constable gives you a description, you might recognise the dead soul."

The constable looked down at the notebook.

"Age about forty, with an angular face – " he commenced.

"That could refer to any of fifty of my patients, Constable," I replied.

" – with a thin hawk-like nose and pointed chin."

"Now, gentlemen, we're down to about twenty-five," I responded, nodding, but I felt my eyes narrowing.

"Lips?" I asked.

"Thin."

"Hairline?"

"Receding."

An icy hand began to clutch at my heart.

"Eyes?"

"Deep-set."

"Colour?"

"Grey."

"My God!" I cried. "Lestrade, those features seem to be pointing to Holmes! Given your grim expression, I fear you agree?"

"I do, Doctor," Lestrade responded. "Especially when the constable tells me the remains are clad in the particular sort of coat Mr. Holmes likes to wear. I can see no alternative but to believe he has been murdered and dismembered."

Without further word, rather than follow the length of the path, the constable forced a way for us through the undergrowth. With whispered apologies to the interred we stumbled over the mounds of long-abandoned graves until at last we came to our destination. It revealed the most terrible sight imaginable. Next to me, Lestrade turned swiftly to the side and was violently sick.

Perched on a grave was the upper body of a man placed as though standing, except the torso had been severed from the legs at the waist. As though anticipating we would push our way through the thicket, the piercing grey eyes were turned towards us. The torso was buttoned into a Prince Albert, a double-breasted frock coat with a flat velvet collar which Holmes would wear on formal occasions and might well decide to wear at his funeral. Pinned to a lapel was a Chevalier degree of the Légion d'Honneur awarded to Holmes by the President of France for his part in the arrest of Huret, the Boulevard Assassin. The coat's skirt extended down only to where the knees would have been, had the legs been left attached. It was a grisly touch. Such flesh as was visible showed the bluish-purple discolouration of Livor mortis, the gravitational settling of blood no longer being pumped through the body after death, a post-mortem sign along with pallor mortis, algor mortis, and rigor mortis. I could hardly bear to look at my old friend, imagining the agony of losing his legs if they had been removed by saw or axe while he still lived. In my fevered brain I half expected to hear the familiar stirring words, “Watson, don’t just stand there gawping! The game’s afoot!” – sending us clattering off across Tower Bridge in yet another hansom cab to new adventures.

I switched my gaze to the incisions on the black granite headstone, plain to see in the bright spring sun. The numerals and lettering were divided into four freshly-cut clusters – a top row over three columns. The row read *District of Birth Yorkshire.* The left column read *Born 6, January 1854. Assassin. Died – Meiringen May 4 in the 58th Year Of The Reign Of Victoria Regina Imperatrix.* The right-hand column read *Place of Birth – Unknown.* The name of the individual being memorialised was displayed in larger lettering on the middle column. Strikingly, the surname *HOLMES* came first, and below it *SHERLOCK.*

My immediate thought was a mistake had been made over the date of death. Clearly Holmes was already dead, yet the date on the stone still had over three weeks to run. My attention turned to what must have been the coup de grâce, a bullet entry through the cadaver’s left temple. There was something remarkably discordant about it, the placement above the ear, the precise shape of a soft-nosed bullet entering the skull at a slight upward angle. I began to move forward for a more forensic examination when a voice from behind me said, “Well, Watson, what do you make of it?”

Lestrade and I turned as one. Before us, with only his torso and head visible in the thicket, dressed in a Prince Albert coat exactly like the Holmes on the slab, stood Holmes himself.

Smiling at our incredulity, he pushed out into the open.

“Don’t worry, gentlemen,” he assured us, chuckling at our expressions, “the real Holmes stands before you, fully bipedal. Mrs. Hudson told me where to find you.”

He pointed at the grave.

“Did you know Ancient Egyptians believed even wax images retain the personality of the dead?”

I turned swiftly to the inspector at my side.

“Lestrade,” I exclaimed, “Can you tell us what else was stolen from the Black Museum in addition to the air-gun? You gave only the briefest account to the newspapers.”

“I can, yes,” Lestrade said, as relieved as I at the sight of my comrade-in-arms. “There are some hundreds of objects on display, many valuable, but the picklocks selected only two – the air-gun, ingeniously adapted by the blind German mechanic to fire soft-nosed bullets which Colonel Sebastian Moran employed that time in trying to kill Mr. Holmes…”

“…and clearly the second object, gentlemen,” Holmes broke in, “was the bust of me which sits upright upon someone else’s decapitated torso on the grave before us, the bust which Moran shot through the left temple with such remarkable accuracy. As you’ll recall, Watson, we gifted both the weapon and the bust to the Black Museum after Moran’s arrest.”

Lestrade nodded.

“Yes, Doctor, just those two objects were taken. This dummy head and the Von Herder air-gun. I’m sure they were stolen to order, just like Gainsborough’s oil of the Duchess of Devonshire nearly twenty years ago and not yet recovered.”

“Just the wax bust and the weapon?” I repeated. I looked across at Lestrade. “Do you have any suspects?”

“Not a one.”

“What does this all mean, Holmes?” I asked. “What are we being told?”

“Do you think there’s a clue over here, Watson?” I heard Holmes asking in a wry tone. He had moved across to a parallel grave only a few feet away. In the same beautifully formed inscriptions, the headstone spelt out on the top row, *West Cork, Ireland*, on the left column, *Died 4 May, 1891, in* *the 54*th *Year Of The Reign Of Victoria Regina Imperatrix*, on the right column, *Eyeries*, ("Presumably the village of the deceased's birth," Holmes remarked), and on the middle column, again in larger lettering than the columns to either side, *MORIARTY* with directly below it *JAMES.*

I knew Eyeries from childhood visits to Ireland, the last village at the end of the beautiful Beara Peninsula.

Was this grave truly the final resting-place of Holmes's archenemy, Professor Moriarty, a man Holmes had once described as the spider at the centre of a criminal web with a thousand threads? It would explain why the Swiss authorities had never pulled his body from the Reichenbach Falls' pit of incalculable depth. Accompanied by the remaining members of Moriarty's gang, Moran could have waited for the body to reappear, even dug a makeshift resting place for it in the sustaining cold of a nearby glacier. The date of death was right. He was thrown into the raging Falls on that day and month four years ago. The day and month inscribed for Holmes's death on the neighbouring headstone would be the exact anniversary in three weeks' time.

I cast my eye at the dense undergrowth surrounding us. Impossible as I knew it to be, what if Colonel Moran, the evil Moriarty's equally malevolent former Chief-of-Staff, was here, on the hunt right now, obsessively seeking revenge for the death of the Professor – for what else could all this rigmarole mean? Even famous hunters like Colonel Julius Barras, devoted to the *shikar* in India and the Nepalese *terai*, acknowledged Moran as the finest Big Game marksman in the Far East. These years later, Moran's bag of tigers was still the record in India. No single British hunter had taken more. Nor was he supreme as a Big Game shot only in the Orient. He had gone on safari in East Africa, leaving the camp one morning with a black powder breech-loading .461 No 1 Gibbs Metford Farquharson single shot rifle and just five cartridges. He returned to Nanyuki with the eight-foot tusks of a bull elephant, the horns of a rhinoceros, the skins of a leopard and a rare black-maned lion, and the massive dense horns of a Cape Buffalo, an animal so dangerous to hunters it was known as "black death".

I looked back at the grisly bust afloat on crimson pools of blood. To entrap Moran, Holmes had placed the startlingly lifelike wax bust by a window at Baker Street, luring the would-be assassin into firing a bullet through its head in the misbelief it was my flesh-and-blood comrade. We lay in wait in an empty house opposite our lodgings and grabbed Moran the moment he fired. My notes recorded –

His eyes had fixed upon Holmes's face with an expression in which hatred and amazement were equally blended.

"You fiend!" he kept on muttering. "You clever, clever fiend!"

"Ah, Colonel!" said Holmes cheerfully, arranging his rumpled collar, "'journeys end in lovers' meetings', as the old play says. I don't think I have had the pleasure of seeing you since you favoured me with those attentions as I lay on the ledge above the Reichenbach Falls."

The remarkable air-gun secured, Moran was carted off to a holding cell near Marble Arch, ready for a first hearing before Magistrate Plowden the next morning. Considered cruel to prolong the wait, he would have been executed for his many murders within the fortnight, but this quickly became notional. To Lestrade's deep embarrassment, a faked-up mêlée by remnants of Moriarty's gang outside the Magistrates Court enabled Moran to escape even before the hearing could take place. The Yard's East End informants tracked him to the docks, by which time he had slipped unnoticed aboard one of any of thirty ships with steam up, all about to leave for far-flung foreign parts.

At the cemetery Holmes broke the brooding silence.

"Does anyone note some oddities about the graves?" he asked. "For example, the headstones?"

"What about them?" I responded.

He pointed towards a nearby cluster of overgrown graves.

"Observe the ones over there. Which direction do they face?"

"Why, east of course, Holmes," I replied, smiling at his apparent lack of knowledge of such matters. "When the Christians' Day of Resurrection comes, the person buried there returns to life and sits bolt upright, directly facing the risen Redeemer coming from the east, as expected."

"And these two headstones? Which direction are they facing?"

"That *is* odd," I replied, staring at them. "They face south."

"Why, do you suppose? Both Moriarty and I were born in Christian countries. This is a Christian burial-ground, not Buddhist or Muslim. There's sufficient space around them for the graves to be dug following the custom of facing east."

"They must have been sited in great haste," I suggested, "and in the dark, not realising the direction the headstones should face to match the others."

"Perhaps," Holmes murmured dubiously. "And yet why the lack of an epitaph on either headstone? Look at the stones over there. '*Time Passes, Memories Remain*' – and that one, Shakespeare's '*To unpathed waters, undreamed shores*'. The Professor was endowed with a phenomenal mathematical faculty. Why not record such an exceptional gift? At the age of twenty-one he wrote a treatise upon the Binomial Theorem which had a European vogue, on the strength of which he won the Mathematical Chair at one of our smaller universities – Marischal College, I believe, where he studied under James Clerk Maxwell."

"I'm afraid I make nothing out of any of this," I replied, adding, "Except to say the calligraphic-style carving is wonderful!"

"Indeed it is," Holmes returned. "Each letter quite beautifully formed."

He turned to the silent but watchful Lestrade.

"Inspector, presumably you made every effort to discover who broke into the Black Museum that night. Did you come across anything unusual?"

"Every effort *was* made, Mr. Holmes, I can assure you," Lestrade replied earnestly. "Not a stone left unturned. Alas, we came up with nothing. Not even how the raiders got away. They disappeared into thin air."

The inspector paused.

"There was one curious matter, a sighting by a passer-by in the early hours of the morning. A rickshaw was standing by some stables in an unlit mews nearby. Rickshaws and pedicabs can legally ply-for-hire on any street, though while they may be a common form of transport with the Chinamen in Poplar, you don't often see 'em along our stretch of the Thames."

At this information Holmes turned back quickly to me. With Lestrade's words, an urgency had suddenly appeared in his demeanour.

"We are in great danger," he informed us. "Until we identify the source, I shall go nowhere without my .450 short-barrelled Webley. Equally, Watson, you must go nowhere without a revolver in a pocket, cocked and ready."

"In great danger!" I parroted incredulously. "From what? A break-in at the Black Museum? A rickshaw standing in the shadows? So what if the graves face south? If you're implying our great enemy Colonel Moran is at the heart of this, surely we've heard the last of him? The newspapers agreed to keep his escape quiet, but Lestrade here has kept us abreast of Moran's movements. If you recall, several sightings have come in over the past few months – admittedly wrong in the case of Sark, but more surely at a Continental port, then Leipzig, then after a gap of several weeks the Scottish archaeologist reported meeting him aboard a shallow-draft steamer on the River Irtish. By now he must be two or three thousand miles from here. All we know is at Imeni Bakhty in Kazakhstan, the trail went cold. I hazard such a circuitous route indicates he has returned to his old haunts in Punjab while deliberately trying to mislead anyone determined to follow him to his destination."

Holmes looked back and forth at the two graves.

"I'm as baffled as both of you," he responded. "As you say, Moran himself cannot be the immediate danger to us right now, but in terrible danger I sense we are, nonetheless."

He paused for a moment. "The break-in at the Black Museum, the headstone for Professor Moriarty, the clear threat to my life 'in the 58th Year of Her Majesty's reign' – all point to the one man, so if Moran isn't hiding in these thickets with Von Herder's gun, nothing makes sense."

He put his two forefingers between his teeth and whistled shrilly, a signal which was answered by a similar whistle from a waiting horse trap. Without offering any further development of his thinking, Holmes set off apace towards the great cedar tree and the exit beyond. Lestrade and I followed in his wake, like dinghies bobbing in the wash of a great ocean liner.

Sotto voce, Lestrade asked me, "Doctor, exactly when *is* the Queen-Empress's fifty-eighth year?"

"We're in it right now," I murmured back. "The would-be assassin must strike very soon if the gravestone is to be an augury."

Part III – We Encounter Mr. Tsang

I was in my chair in the sitting room the next morning when Holmes came bounding up the stairs. He was clad in clothing bought from an old clothes shop in Stepney for his more inconspicuous visits to 'Darkest London'. It was from there he was returning, in the frayed jacket with one remaining button, the well-worn but stout trousers, and the pair of brogans which had plainly seen service where coal was shovelled. On his head was a very dirty cloth cap which he threw expertly on to the hat-stand. He was positively wriggling with excitement.

"Success!" he cried out. "Watson, we find ourselves in the midst of a very remarkable inquiry. The chappie we're looking for is Mr. Tsang Wing Ma. Tsang is the family name. He's a community scribe of high standing, famed for his exceptional skill in the centuries-old practice of Chinese calligraphy. We must pay him a visit at Toynbee Hall, unannounced.

"I spent the night," he continued, "in Ah Sing's on Upper Swandam Lane. That opium den is the vilest murder-trap on the whole riverside, but as a source of information it's nonpareil. Once inside the building, I had to tread carefully. An electric bell under the floor acts as a warning system, and progress through the house is obstructed by a set of stout oak panels, ropes and pulleys, levers, and a trapdoor at the top of the stairs. Even then, the opium-smoking room has to be accessed by clambering out on to a sloping roof and climbing back into the property through a skylight. We should be rich men if we had a thousand pounds for every poor devil who's been done to death in that sordid, squalid place. Had I been recognised at any stage of my passage through the house, my life wouldn't have been worth an hour's purchase."

I waited expectantly as he threw himself into his chair, warming his hands in front of the coal fire.

"I suppose," he continued, smiling, "you imagine I've added opium-smoking to my seven-per-cent solutions of cocaine and all the other little weaknesses on which you favour me with your medical views."

"More to the point, Holmes, why a Chinese scribe?" I asked. "What's that to do with the headstones? Why should Chinese calligraphy be of any concern to us?"

I pointed at the calendar over the mantel.

"Must I remind you" I continued, "that you may only have twenty-one days and counting to live?"

"It has very little to do with Chinese calligraphy *per se*," came the cryptic answer, "though a very great deal to do with the inscriptions on the two headstones."

Holmes reached into the frayed jacket and pulled out a slim volume.

"Last night I took the chance to visit several bookshops in Limehouse and Poplar. This is a book on Chinese gravestones, especially those from the region north of the Yangtze and south of the River Huai. The Chinese community in London likes to keep to their ancient traditions surrounding death, you see."

"Holmes!" I burst out, snorting with laughter. "Why on Earth would you want to learn about – " At which Holmes passed the book to me.

"Page eight, please," he ordered. "Note the pictures of gravestones. Does anything about them strike you as interesting?"

I studied each of several pictures and looked up.

"I'm sorry. All I can see are headstones covered with Chinese characters. What connection could there possibly be between the nature of headstones found between the Yangtze and the – (I looked back at the page) – Huai, and the headstones at the cemetery?"

In a decidedly mocking tone, Holmes replied, "Gentlemen of the jury, yet again we have an example of my amanuensis *seeing* but proving he is not *observing*! Watson, look at the *pattern* of the logograms on the Chinese headstones. Both you and our Scotland Yard friend Lestrade failed to notice that while the wording on the two headstones at Highgate Cemetery was in English – like all the other gravestones – the *lay-out* on Moriarty's and mine was classical Chinese. The row across the top, the three columns under it, the middle column in larger characters. Even the family name first, the given name beneath. As to why Mr. Tsang, he is a Chinese scribe, and you yourself admired the sheer beauty of the lettering on the two stones. They must have been inscribed by a mason under the tutelage of a scribe of the highest reputation. Then when Lestrade told us about the rickshaw waiting in the dark near the Black Museum – "

Holmes got to his feet.

"I admit this is a most mystifying case. Unless we can forestall violent forces set against us, it's a case which may truly end with my death on the fourth of May. In fact, my great friend, I urge you to compose an authentic epitaph for me, just in case – perhaps including some reference to my life's work."

"How about something like '*Universally Considered the Most Famous Consulting Detective of His Day*'?" I asked impishly, testing the extent of his modesty.

He looked back from the door to his quarters. "Yes, that might do. Have it inscribed over the Shakespearean elegy we saw at the Cemetery – '*To unpathed waters, undreamed shores*'. I tell you, Watson, while your *métier* is action and not thought, your questioning has caused a most unexpected idea to form in my mind, a scenario which includes the elusive Moran, but partnered by a malignance far in excess of our usual East End river pirates and scuffle-hunters. Truly my life may depend on what we can learn from Mr. Tsang."

As he left the room he called back, "I don't wish to be interrupted. To work this out I shall need five pillows and at least an ounce of shag."

Over the next several days our minds were preoccupied with a case I was eventually to publish under the title '*The Solitary Cyclist*'. Holmes brought the matter to a satisfactory conclusion, and we were able to return to the thread in his life so clearly carved into the headstone at Highgate Cemetery. Thus we found ourselves rattling towards the East End, squeezed together in a hansom, the Webley Mark-IV Top-Breaker six-shot revolver in .476 calibre in my inner pocket. Holmes was looking pensive. As always, he was continuing his infuriating penchant of springing surprises rather than taking me into his confidence.

With an impressive "Whoa!" the cabbie brought us to a halt outside Toynbee Hall. The building's resemblance to a manorial residence in Elizabethan style stood out in a neighbourhood full of cramped slum housing. Once inside, Holmes gave our adopted pseudonyms and asked where we could locate the eminent Chinese community scribe Tsang Wing Ma. He was, we were informed, to be found in the drawing room, an elaborate chamber decorated with eastern rugs and Oriental-style wall hangings. Mr. Tsang stood up and bowed as we entered. He was formally attired in a one-piece dress worn by scholar-officials as far back as the Song Dynasty. On noting my interest, he explained the four panels of fabric making up the upper part represented the four seasons, the lower twelve panels the number of months in the year. He gave a sweep of his arm, inviting us to a black lacquer mother-of-pearl sofa.

"How may I help you, gentlemen?" he asked.

“We are here to consult you in your professional capacity,” Holmes began portentously. “My friend here is an eminent doctor. Among his patients is an Englishman who is dying, a man of standing who made his considerable fortune in the Orient – in China. The poor fellow has no living relatives. He has little time left. He has begged us to order his headstone. He wants the inscriptions to be laid out in the Chinese style, the top row over three columns and so on. Hence our presence here.”

Holmes paused, his hands held forward in a disarming manner.

“Is that something you are able to design – your work fully remunerated of course?”

“That is part of my service to the Chinese community,” the Chinaman responded. “Tell me, do you want the inscriptions drafted in traditional Chinese – Cantonese or Mandarin perhaps?”

Holmes’s hands rose.

“No,” he said solemnly, “our dying friend merely wishes the *format* to remind people of his years in China. The wording itself he wants in English.”

I had been looking back and forth between my companion and the man before us, nodding in agreement as Holmes laid out the cock-and-bull story. My eyes were on the scribe at the moment Holmes ended his explanation. Had the Chinaman’s eyes narrowed suddenly? Had his earlier relaxed posture stiffened? He had been attentive in a friendly way until Holmes explained “our dying friend” wanted the lettering laid out in the Chinese style but “the wording itself he wants in English”. Certainly the scribe’s eyes were now locked unwaveringly on Holmes. The brush dropped from his fingers. He got quickly to his feet and sped across to the window. He gave a quick glance into the open roadway.

He turned back to face us.

"Gentlemen," he said, "I am sorry I cannot be of help. If I understand truly why you are here, I must ask you to leave at once, please – never to return."

Without further ado, he crossed swiftly to the door and left the chamber.

Holmes said, "As you saw, Watson, my suspicions are correct. He fled fearing for his life."

The fourth of the month was fast approaching. As far as I could see, Holmes was making no further advances in the case of the two headstones. Then, on a morning Mrs. Hudson brought a tray with another fine breakfast – ham and eggs, followed by curried mutton and her family heirloom, the magnificent, silver-plated coffee pot – Holmes again disappeared. I was taking the meal alone. The dishes were accompanied by a further copy of *The Echo*. A small piece on a back page announced *From our Woolwich Correspondent. Chinaman Found Drowned. Possible Suicide*. I put down my knife and fork.

> *In the early hours of this morning, the corpse of a Chinaman was dragged from the Thames at Woolwich by the ferryboat* Hutton, *a side-loading paddle-steamer. Identification will be difficult as it is not known where the man entered the water. The tidal flow may have brought him down-river from the St. Katherine Docks or Limehouse Wharf area. The deceased was dressed in a* 'shenyi', *a traditional if outmoded Chinese men's outfit made from bleached linen. Both wrists had been slashed, severing the tendons, though death appears to have been from drowning, weighed down by his garment, rather than exsanguination. No investigation into the tragedy will take place. The river police at Wapping have taken it to be a clear case of suicide.*

I put the newspaper down. If, as I felt sure, this was Tsang, it was too much of a coincidence for his death to have been anything but the outcome of our visit. Why on Earth had we so heedlessly barged in on the scribe, and in broad daylight? What foul agency had sliced through the *flexor carpi* of both wrists, rendering useless a heaven-sent prowess without which the scribe's *raison d'être* was destroyed? As Assistant Surgeon at the terrible battle of Maiwand in 1880, I had seen the effect of a sword slash across a wrist raised defensively. The hand becomes functionally inoperable. Did the fiends slash the tendons and leave it to Tsang himself to decide he could no longer face life, unable ever again to perform the brushstrokes for his beautiful logograms? Was his drowning a suicide – in effect *murder*?

I was deep in meditation over the now ever-more credible threat to Holmes's life when I heard our housekeeper calling up the stairway. With the passing years, she was less inclined to take on the steps except to bring us our meals. I opened the door to the landing and called down, "Yes, I'm still here, Mrs. Hudson. If you're bringing up today's post, may I ask for a further pot of your excellent Java coffee, please?"

Ten minutes later, she came through the door with the coffee and a letter on a salver. It was addressed to me. Even before I looked at the signature, I knew from the Xuan paper and the several sublime logograms in lampblack ink it was from Mr. Tsang.

Dear Dr. Watson, (he began)

As I feared, the secret society was keeping watch over my visitors to Toynbee Hall. They recognised you and Mr. Holmes. Therefore this will be the last letter I shall be able to write. I have only a short time left before outriders of the

Green Gang (青幫) will come for me. To themselves, they are known as 'Friends Of The Way of Tranquillity and Purity' *(or 安清道友) but violence is their major trait. Their rituals include ancestral worship, astral worship, Taoism, Buddhism, and Confucianism. Their common aim is to avenge the Five Ancestors by bringing about the overthrow of the Qing Dynasty and the restoration of the Ming.*

They assumed I invited you to meet to reveal that the plot written into the headstones which – I assume you have already calculated – involves Professor Moriarty's former Chief of Staff, Colonel Moran. I have now been informed of the fate awaiting me, the same punishment they threatened if I refused to design the headstones. They will sever the wrist-joint tendons with a cutlass so I can never move a brush across the paper ever again. Second, they will lock me standing in an iron cage known as a water dungeon, to be lowered into a tank until the water level reaches my neck. Very quickly I shall become cold. Unable to sit or sleep, I shall become unconscious and drown.

However, it can be said that before a man embarks on a journey of revenge, he should dig two graves, in this case the one for me but the other for the Green Gang. Hence this letter to you.

The westerly of the two gravestones speaks for itself. It is an affirmation Professor Moriarty died at the Reichenbach Falls (at the hands of Mr. Sherlock Holmes) on that date – nothing more, though it implies retribution is required. The easterly stone reveals much more. By being placed next to the Professor's grave, it threatens Mr. Holmes with revenge – namely a similar fate for toppling Professor Moriarty to his death, which in Chinese we depict as

报应，天谴；应得的惩罚；不可避免的失败

This is 'a cause of punishment or defeat that is deserved and cannot be avoided', *to be carried out on the anniversary of the same day and month that Professor Moriarty died.*

I now come to how the plot to kill Mr. Holmes will play out through an agreement between the Green Gang and Colonel Moran. By now, the Colonel will be –

Suddenly the clear writing turned into scribble.

They are here. Three rickshaws have arrived together. my life is about to return to the Yellow Springs.

寿比南山 (May you live as long as Southern mountain).

Tsang Wing Ma

I went across to the window and looked down at the rows of cabs. The letter confirmed a murderous secret society was involved, one reported to rely on magical charms to ward off bullets. As wretched bad luck would have it, just five more minutes and Tsang would have given us the details of the plot.

Again and again I went over our encounter with the scribe and the way it had ended so abruptly. The death could only have been our fault, Holmes's and mine. When we departed that day I looked back and saw him watching us. Again and again the expression on his face came back to me as he stood looking out of a window. If ever a man wore an expression of abject resignation, it was Tsang's at that moment. Surely we should have foretold he had been pressed by a merciless element into devising the headstones. There would therefore be consequences in our visit. It wasn't long after Holmes began offering a most unlikely reason for being there that Tsang himself realised it was Holmes settled on the sofa couch, with me at his side. By then, for Tsang, it was too late.

Holmes returned early that evening. First I showed him the cutting from *The Echo*. He read it carefully. Then I handed him Tsang's letter, saying "It is you and I who dug his grave". He read the letter and looked up with an expression of excitement, waving it in the air.

"They made a blunder of the first water!" he exclaimed. "The realisation they would murder him provoked Tsang's letter to us. They may have dug a grave for him, but he has dug a second grave – for them!"

Confounded, I asked, "How has he done that? He was interrupted right when he was going to reveal the plot against you. The letter tells us nothing. Worse, he wasted precious minutes writing about an oath the Gang imposed on initiates, the one swearing to avenge the Five Ancestors and bring about the overthrow of the Qing Dynasty and the restoration of the Ming. What has that to do with anything?"

"You say Tsang wasted precious minutes," Holmes replied. "I say he did not. That oath is the very clue we needed to solve the puzzle – it answers the question - How can Moran murder me on the fourth if he's thousands of miles away?."

He led me quickly to the terrestrial globe next to the grandfather clock.

"Watson, show me where Moran was last spotted before the trail went cold."

I spun the globe to the vast stretches of Central Asia.

"Here," I said. "Imeni Bakhty in Kazakhstan."

I ran my finger down the globe.

"Probably pretending to be an archaeologist," I resumed, "he will have turned south and taken this route, through Bishkek and Dyushambe, and onward to his old stamping-grounds in Punjab."

"He may have assumed the profession of archaeology," Holmes replied, "but it wasn't south to Punjab he was going."

Nonplussed, I asked, "Then where? Are you suggesting he turned around completely and will soon be back among us?"

"I am not," Holmes replied.

His finger replaced mine on the globe.

"This way. This is the way he's going."

His bony finger ran directly eastward.

"By now he'll have reached Sinkiang," he added.

"Sinkiang!" I echoed. "But that's in China!"

"My old friend,' Holmes replied, smiling at my puzzlement, "remember what Tsang has just told us of the 'Friends of the Way of Tranquillity and Purity'? To work for the overthrow of the ruling Qing Dynasty, sometimes called the Manchu Dynasty, and the reinstatement of the Ming regime? The secret books of the Green Gang would reveal they continue with that goal unabated by time. Moran's destination isn't Punjab. It's the Forbidden City."

"The Forbidden City!" I cried. "So what exactly *is* Moran's part? Why is he in China? He can hardly kill you from there!"

"He can't, but he can have me killed through an ineffably cunning *quid pro quo*," Holmes replied. "Nothing less than by assassinating the Manchu Dowager Empress Cixi herself, sparking a Han uprising against the Qing and a restoration of the Ming. The moment news comes that he has succeeded in murdering her, the Green Gang will kidnap me, transport me back to Meiringen and the Reichenbach Falls in time for the fourth of May. Moran will have drawn them a map. Four years ago, from high in the cliffs above, he observed the struggle. At the exact hour I pitched Moriarty into the roiling waters, they'll hurl me, alive, from the same ledge into the depths, fulfilling the fate ascribed to me on my headstone at Highgate Cemetery."

Part IV – We Meet the Foreign Secretary

After a restless night, I awoke to the sound of voices from our sitting room on the floor below. I dressed and hurried down. Holmes was in his customary chair at the fireside. He was talking to Inspector Lestrade and a well-dressed man of middle age. The latter's face was familiar.

"Watson," Holmes said, "Lestrade you know well. You may recognise our other guest. He is John Wodehouse, 1st Earl of Kimberley."

"I do recognise him," I replied, stepping forward to shake hands. "England's Secretary of State for Foreign Affairs."

"At least for a few more weeks, Dr. Watson," the Earl replied. "After June, I shall be out of office."

"June is long enough," Holmes intervened. He waved a hand at Mrs. Hudson's silver-plated coffee pot placed precariously over a spirit-lamp on the chemical bench. "Help yourself, Watson, and bring a chair and join us. We've finished discussing the weather and are now deciding what to do about Moran's imminent arrival in Peking. As Foreign Secretary, the Earl has his own house of cards to play."

"Mr. Holmes is right," the Foreign Secretary agreed. "There's a very considerable wish among Her Britannic Majesty's Cabinet to rebuild the promising relations we had with the Empress Dowager Cixi some years ago when she appeared open to diplomatic incursions, until her attitude towards foreigners changed. Last year, China was heavily defeated in the war with Japan. China's entire fleet of battleships was wiped out, and Cixi humiliated. She needs powerful friends. We believe the present time is opportune. Our trade, such as it remains, is concentrated at the treaty ports. Interior China is still *terra incognita* to our traders. By no means does the British Government wish for a return of the Ming. Colonel Moran could be a very timely pawn. We could start the process of ingratiation by informing Cixi of Colonel Moran's advance on the Forbidden City and the likely weapon he'll be carrying."

The Foreign Secretary gave a shudder.

"Heaven knows what they'll do to him. They may drive sharp bamboo sticks underneath the fingernails with a hammer. While they start off with one finger, sometimes all fingers are "treated". He would never be able to pull a trigger again. They might then pass him to the *Daozi jiang*, the knifer responsible for castrations. I'm told the local anaesthetic they use is hot chilli sauce. Or he might suffer the appalling death they call *Lingchi*, 'Death by a Thousand Cuts'. Fortunately we don't need to be told."

An hour later a decision was reached. I was to supply a physical description of our old enemy to be collected the same evening by special envoy and sent to the Dowager Empress via "our man" in Peking. The *entente* included an unusual but firm stipulation made by Holmes over Moran's fate, to which the Earl agreed. We toasted Her Imperial Majesty, England's Great Queen, with a cobwebby Margaux 1890 brought up to us by Mrs. Hudson from her cellar.

I looked back for the description I made a year earlier when we captured Moran and his remarkable air-gun: '*It was a tremendously virile and yet sinister face which was turned towards us…one could not look upon his cruel blue eyes, with their drooping, cynical lids, or upon the fierce, aggressive nose and the threatening, deep-lined brow, without reading Nature's plainest danger-signals.*'

I would accompany the description with a sketch of the air-gun.

The following day Holmes volunteered to accompany me on my after-lunch walk to the Regent's Park to observe the heron which had recently taken up residence on the lake. We settled ourselves on a favourite bench.

"Holmes," I began, "before we go any further in our conversation, I want an explanation from you. At yesterday's discussion with the Earl of Kimberley, you called for a particular proviso, that Her Majesty's government should insist on a promise from the Empress Dowager *not* to execute Moran, but instead imprison him under close guard and only for a period of ten years. The Foreign Secretary went along with that. I ask, why not simply have done with it – have Moran executed? The Green Gang will not pursue you if Moran fails to live up to his side of the *quid pro quo*, but left alive he might escape, no matter how he's locked up and no matter how many eunuchs are assigned to guard him. Your life would again be at terrible risk. Call in on the Earl tomorrow. Say that on reflection you've changed your mind, that given you once called Moran the second-most dangerous person in London, after Moriarty, you would have no qualms if he's executed within days of being captured. It doesn't have to be *Lingchi* – it could be a straight-forward decapitation with a sharp sword. Surely that would be best for the world?"

"My dear comrade-in-arms," came the reply, "my life as a consulting detective has become singularly uninteresting since Professor Moriarty's abrupt departure. Ten years from now I may be on the point of retiring to write my magnum opus, *The Whole Art Of Detection*. Already I have in mind a bee-farm on the Sussex Downs. And then Moran returns. I have no doubt he will have spent his time in a dungeon in the Forbidden City hatching a most diabolical plot to avenge his master. Think what a fresh great game would be afoot!"

"Then I hope you'll invite me to join in!" I exclaimed.

"Yes, my old friend," came the welcome reply, "you have my word."

The End

NOTES

The fiendish Colonel Sebastian Moran did return, in another of my short stories titled 'A Most Diabolical Plot'. The Colonel returns from China's Forbidden City even more determined to seek revenge on Holmes. 'A Most Diabolical Plot' is in *The MX Book of New Sherlock Holmes Stories – Part III*, and in a book of my short stories with the overall title 'A Most Diabolical Plot'.

Mrs. Hudson. 'Our housekeeper Mrs. Hudson came up the stairs, bringing me a fine breakfast in the Scotch style -' Watson was particularly fond of the landlady-cum-housekeeper. In 'The Adventure of the Dying Detective' he writes, she '*was a long-suffering woman. Not only was her first-floor flat invaded at all hours by throngs of singular and often undesirable characters but her remarkable lodger (Holmes) showed an eccentricity and irregularity in his life which must have sorely tried her patience. His incredible untidiness, his addiction to music at strange hours, his occasional revolver practice within doors, his weird and often malodorous scientific experiments, and the atmosphere of violence and danger which hung around him made him the very worst tenant in London.*'

Shikar. The hunt, especially Big Game hunting during the Raj.

'Cape Buffalo, an animal so dangerous to hunters it was known as "black death".' I know what Watson meant by this description. My own first job was as an assistant-manager on a very large farm high up on the slopes of Mt. Kenya with every imaginable Big Game animal around, including herds of Cape Buffalo. Even Professional hunters learnt to respect them or get badly injured or killed.

The Whole Art Of Detection. Holmes told Watson "Ten years from now I may be on the point of retiring to write my magnum opus, *The Whole Art Of Detection".* Holmes did retire to a bee-farm on the Sussex Downs around 1904. However, in 'His Last Bow', alas for the world of criminology, it was reported he published *'The practical handbook of bee culture: with some observations upon the segregation of the queen'* instead.

ACKNOWLEDGEMENTS

Professor Judith Rowbotham, for her extraordinary knowledge of Ancient China, in addition to her specialism in Victorian crime and punishment.
Dr. Ian Dungavell, Friends of Highgate Cemetery Trust. To discover who is buried there go to https://highgatecemetery.org/visit/searches but keep in mind 170,000 people are buried there in 53,000 graves, including over 300 War graves.
Paul Bickley, Curator, Crime Museum, New Scotland Yard. Known as the Black Museum until the early 21st century, the museum came into existence at Scotland Yard sometime in 1874, arising out of the collection of prisoners' property gathered as a result of the Forfeiture Act 1870 and intended as an aid to the police in their study of crime and criminals.

Research material.

The Evolution of The Luo Teaching And The Formation Of The Green Gang. Abstract by Ma Xisha.
East End Chronicles, by Ed Glinnert. Allen Lane.

The Mystery Of the Missing Artefacts

Location: *A dungeon under the Dolmabahçe Palace, Constantinople. August 1916*

I stared up at the patch of blue sky visible through a tiny grille high up on the wall. I was a prisoner-of-war in Constantinople, left to rot in a dank cell under the magnificent State rooms of Sultan Mehmed V Reşâd's Palace, my only distraction a much-thumbed copy of Joseph Conrad's *The Secret Agent*. Near-permanent pangs of hunger endlessly recalled a fine meal I enjoyed with my old friend Sherlock Holmes at London's famous Grand Cigar Divan restaurant some years earlier. What I would now give for such a repast, I reflected unhappily. As can happen in extreme isolation, every detail came to mind - the Chef walking imposingly alongside the lesser mortal propelling a silver dinner wagon, Holmes ordering slices of beef carved from large joint, with a portion of fat. I chose the smoked salmon, a signature dish of the establishment. For dessert, we decided upon the famous treacle sponge with a dressing of Madagascan vanilla custard. And a Trichinopoly cigar to top it off.

I should explain how twists and turns of fate had brought me to my present state. I shall not go into exhaustive detail. It is irrelevant to the bizarre case soon to unravel in a small market town in the English county of Sussex. Suffice it to say that, at the start of the war against the German Kaiser and his Ottoman ally, I volunteered to rejoin my old Regiment. Instead, the Army Medical Corps assigned me to the 6th (Poona) Division of the British Indian Army, which had captured the town of Kut-al-Amara a hundred miles south of Baghdad, in the heart of Mesopotamia. I had hardly taken up my post when the Sultan retaliated by ordering his troops to besiege us.

Five desperate months left us entirely without food or potable water. Our Commanding Officer surrendered. The victors separated British Field Officers from Indian Other Ranks and transported us to various camps across the Ottoman Empire. I found myself delivered to the very palace where, ten years earlier, the previous ruler, Sultan Abd-ul-Hamid II, received Sherlock Holmes and me as honoured guests.[1] Now I was confined to a dungeon under the two-hundred-eighty-five rooms, forty-six halls, six *hamams*, and sixty-eight toilets of the magnificent building. It was clear from the despairing cries of my fellow captives that I was to be left in squalor and near-starvation until the Grim Reaper came to take me to The Life Beyond.

The heavy door of my cell swung open. Rather than the surly Turkish warder bringing a once-daily bowl of watery grey soup, a visitor from the outside world stood there. We stared at each other. I judged him to be an American from the three-button jacket with long rolling lapels and shoulders free of padding. The four-button cuffs and military high-waisted effect reflected the influence of the American serviceman's uniform on civilian fashion.

The visitor spoke first. "Captain Watson, M.D. I presume?" he asked cordially. He had a New England accent.

"At your service," I said warily, getting to my feet. I was embarrassed by the tattered state of my British Indian Army uniform and Service Dress hat. "And you might be?"

Hand outstretched, the visitor stepped into the cell. "Mr. Philip," he replied. "American Embassy. A Diplomatic courier came from England with a telegram for you. I apologise for the time it's taken to discover your whereabouts. At the American Embassy we are all acquainted with the crime stories in *The Strand* magazine written by Sherlock Holmes's great friend, Dr. John H. Watson. None of us realised the Ottoman prisoner of war 'Captain' Watson was one and the same." The emissary's gaze flickered around, suppressing any change of expression at the fetid air. The pestilential hole had been my home-from-home for more than a month. "Not the finest quarters for a British officer, are they?" he smiled sympathetically.

I pointed impatiently at the small envelope in his hand. "Is that the telegram?" I prompted. Mr. Philip handed it to me with a nod. The envelope carried the words '*From Sherlock Holmes, for the Attention of Captain Watson MD, Constantinople. To be delivered by hand.*'

"I have no doubt," Mr. Philip went on, "that it's to inform you your old companion is working energetically through the Powers-that-Be to have you released and returned to England."

Nodding agreement, I tore open the envelope. My jaw dropped. I glanced up at my visitor and returned my disbelieving gaze to the telegram. "*My dear Watson,*" I read again, "*Do you remember the name of the fellow at the*

British Museum who contacted us over a certain matter just before I retired to my bee-farm in the South Downs?"

I remembered the matter in considerable detail. Towards the end of 1903, a letter marked *Urgent & Confidential* arrived at Holmes's Baker Street quarters. It was from a Michael Lacey, Keeper of Antiquities at the British Museum. Some dozens of small items in the Ancient and Mediaeval Battlefield department had gone missing, artefacts ploughed up on ancient battlegrounds or retrieved from graves of tenth or eleventh Century English knights and bowmen. They were of no intrinsic value. The artefacts had spent some years in storage awaiting archiving, but due to a shortage of experts no work had been carried out. Would Mr. Holmes come to see the Keeper at the Museum and investigate their disappearance? Holmes waved dismissively. "Probably an inside job – perhaps a floor-sweeper hoping to augment a pitiful salary. It would hardly prove even a one-Abdulla-cigarette problem." My comrade clambered to his feet, reached for his Inverness cape and announced, "I plan to spend today at my bee-farm on the Sussex Downs, checking my little workers are doing what Nature designed for them, filling jars with a golden liquid purloined from the buttercup, the poppy, and the Blue Speedwell."

He looked back from the door. "Watson, don't look so crestfallen. It's hardly as if the umbra of Professor Moriarty of evil memory has marched in and stolen the Elgin Marbles. Kindly inform this Keeper of Antiquities that I haven't the faintest interest in the matter. Refer him to any Jack-in-office at Scotland Yard." His voice floated back up from the stairwell. "No doubt Inspector Lestrade will happily take time away from chasing horse-flies in Surrey to check on an owl job of such little consequence." With a shout to our housekeeper of "Good day, Mrs. Hudson!" Holmes stepped into the bustle of Baker Street and was gone.

Now, inexplicably, ten and more years into retirement, he wanted to know the man's name. Not one word on my desperate situation. I turned the telegram over and wrote,

'*Dear Holmes, the name of the Keeper at the British Museum was Michael Lacey. Why do you ask? I recall how rudely you refused to take up the case. You said that after 'A Scandal in Bohemia', no ordinary burglary could ever be of interest to you.*'

With blistering sarcasm I added, '*Would you do me a small favour? When you can find a moment away from whatever you're pursuing, get me out of here as quickly as possible? If the rancid slop doesn't do for me, cholera will.*'

The days passed with agonising slowness. At last, Mr. Philip returned. He told me the American Ambassador would shortly be making a demarche to the Sublime Porte to get me released. He handed me a second communication from England. I wrenched it open. The envelope contained a cutting from a Sussex newspaper, *The Battle Observer*. Below an advertisement for the Central Picture Theatre (*The Folly of Youth*), Holmes had marked out a photograph of a corpse lying in a field below ancient ruins. The photograph was attributed to a Brian Hanson, using a Sinclair Una De Luxe No. 2 – a camera I was myself planning to purchase using the savings from my Army pay forced on me by my incarceration. The headline blared '*Strange Death of Former British Museum Keeper*'.

The report continued -

> *Early this morning a body was discovered by local resident Mrs. Johnson walking her dog across the site of the Battle of Hastings. An arrow jutted out of the deceased's left eye. The dead man has been identified as Michael Lacey, former Head of Antiquities at the British Museum. The police were called, and the body removed to the Union Workhouse hospital. It is not known what*

the deceased was doing in the field in the night. It is a spot seldom frequented after dark. Local legend holds the land runs crimson with blood when the rain falls. Ghostly figures have made appearances – phantom monks and spectral knights, red and grey ladies. Furthermore, each October, on the eve of the famous battle, a lone ghostly knight has been reported riding soundlessly across the battlefield.

The article ended -

The police describe Mr. Lacey as a well-known if controversial and isolated figure in the area since his retirement to a house on Caldbec Hill over ten years ago. He was rumoured to hold to the widely discredited theory that the Battle between William of Normandy and Harold Godwinson of England did not take place on the slopes below the present-day ruins of Battle Abbey, but at a location several miles away. What remains certain is that William's victory and Harold's death from an arrow in the eye changed the course of our Island's history, laws, and customs.

An accompanying note in Holmes's scrawl said, '*Come soonest. SH.*'

A week later, a Turkish Major-General fell into the hands of British forces outside Jerusalem. A prisoner-exchange was agreed. By early October, I was back in London, greeting the locum at my Marylebone surgery. In a matter of hours, the Chinese laundry on Tottenham Court Road restored my Indian Army uniform, topee and Sam Browne belt to pristine condition. I would wear the uniform for my visit to Holmes to avoid the accusation of cowardice from the ladies of the Order of the White Feather.

I tarried further in the Capital just long enough to visit Solomon's in Piccadilly to purchase a supply of black hothouse grapes, and Salmon and Gluckstein of Oxford Street where I stocked up with a half-a-dozen tins of J&H Wilson No. 1 Top Mill Snuff and several boxes of Trichinopoly cigars. The train deposited me at Eastbourne. I boarded a sturdy four-wheeler to engage with the mud.

The ancient County of Sussex is rich in historical features and archaeological remains, including defensive sites, burial mounds, and field boundaries. Holmes's bee-farm was tucked in rolling chalk downland with close-cropped turf and dry valleys stretching from the Itchen Valley in the west to Beachy Head in the east. Some miles later a lonely, low-lying black-and-white building with a stone courtyard and crimson ramblers came into view. Holmes was waiting to greet me. At the familiar sight a wave of nostalgia washed through me.

While I fumbled for money to pay the cabman, Holmes drummed his fingers on the side of the carriage. The payment made, at a touch of the driver's whip the horses wheeled and turned away. Holmes reached a hand across to my shoulder. "Well done, Watson," he said, adding in the sarcastic tone of old, "Prompt as ever in answering a telegraphic summons."

"Holmes!" I cried. "You might remember I was rotting in a dungeon in the Sultan's Palace two thousand miles away when your invitation arrived. I was lucky to find a British warship in Alexandria, or I might have been incarcerated a second time. The Mediterranean bristles with the Kaiser's dreadnoughts and battlecruisers."

To mollify me, Holmes said, "We must ask my housekeeper, Mrs. Keppler, to bring you a restorative cup of tea. You will be offered a very civilised choice of shiny black tea or scented green."

We seated ourselves in the Summerhouse. I handed over the tray of Solomon's black grapes and a share of the Trichinopoly cigars. My comrade passed across a large copy of the newspaper picture I had first seen in the Turkish cell. "I obtained this at a modest charge from *The Battle Observer*," he explained. "Now, Watson, you're a medical chap. I need your help. My knowledge of anatomy is accurate, but unsystematic. Tell me, what do you think?"

"Think about what precisely?" I queried, staring at the corpse in the picture.

"The arrow in his eye," came Holmes's reply. "The local police say he must done it to himself," he continued. "King Harold was shot in the eye by a Norman arrow. They suggest Lacey chose to die the same death, maddened by his failure to disprove the true site of the battle. The citizens of the town are in a hurry to close the case. They most definitely do not wish for unfavourable publicity ahead of the commemorative events."

"Which events?" I asked.

"The eight-hundred-and-fiftieth anniversary of the Battle of Hastings," Holmes replied. "In a week's time. Hundreds of visitors are expected. *Le Tout-Battle* wishes to make a windfall from them."

"If you mean did the arrow cause his death, I can answer that straight away, Holmes. No, the arrow was not the cause of Lacey's death. The angle of entry is quite wrong. It would have slipped past any vital part of the brain. In Afghanistan I administered to one of our Indian troops who caught an arrow in the eye. He lived on for months and probably years."

"Could it have been self-inflicted?" Holmes asked.

"Unlikely," I replied. "In my opinion, he was already dead when the arrow was pushed into his eye."

Holmes asked, "So the fear and horror on his face?"

"Already frozen into it."

"Therefore the real cause of death?"

"Undoubtedly a heart attack," I replied. "From fright," I opined. "Something spine-chilling must have happened to Lacey on that isolated spot. Whatever it was, a rush of adrenaline stunned his cardiac muscle into inaction. Think of Colonel Barclay's death in the matter of 'the Crooked Man'. He died of fright. There's a close similarity here. Dying of fright is a rather more frequent medical condition than you may imagine. I estimate one person a day dies from it in any of our great cities."

Holmes rose quickly. "You have me intrigued, Watson. We must hurry. Drink up your tea. I may not have displayed the slightest interest in the Keeper of Antiquities and his little problems while he was alive, but in death he presents a most unusual case."

"Hurry where?" I asked, bewildered.

"Why, to the British Museum, where else! It'll be like old times. The last time I was there, I read up on voodooism."

We went into the house. Holmes picked up the telephone receiver to order a cab. As we waited, he remarked, "A small point but one of interest, Watson. The police outside London often asked for my assistance whenever I was in the neighbourhood. I am a mere twenty miles from Battle. The inspector knows I am here, yet despite a mysterious death on his patch, no request to meet me has arrived at my door. What do you make of that?"

Within the quarter-hour a carriage arrived. As we jolted along, Holmes pulled out a packet of Pall Mall Turkish cigarettes and lit one, eyes narrowing against the smoke. He reached into his voluminous coat for the photographic print purchased from *The Battle Observer*. He stared at the image, puffing in thoughtful silence. "What is it, Holmes?" I asked at last. "Why the knitted brow and repeated drumming on your knee?"

"There's something odd here, Watson. Something I quite missed at first. You have my copy of *The Observer* in your side-pocket. Can you pass it to me, please?" Holmes reached once more into his coat, withdrawing a ten-power silver-and-chrome magnifying glass. For a while it hovered over the newspaper. I was once again irresistibly reminded of a well-trained foxhound dashing back and forth through the covert, whining in its eagerness until it comes across the lost scent.

Holmes gave a grunt. He passed the print and magnifying glass to me. "Tell me what you see," he ordered. I stared down through the powerful glass.

"Nothing unusual, Holmes," I said, looking up.

Holmes asked, "What about the grass under the corpse's head?"

"The ground around the body gives no indication of a deadly struggle," I replied. "Is that what you mean?"

He passed the newspaper back to me and commanded, "Now look again at the grass around the body as it appears in *The Observer*."

Once more I looked through the magnifying glass. "Why, it's nowhere near as clear as in the print, Holmes," I replied. "In fact it's quite grainy."

"Precisely, my dear fellow. Why would the grass be quite clearly defined in the print but look grainy when the same photograph appears in the newspaper? This is a three-pipe problem at the very least, Watson. I beg you not to speak to me for fifty minutes."

Holmes flicked the cigarette butt out of the carriage window and produced his favourite blackened briar. I threw my tobacco pouch to his side and looked quickly out of the carriage window, blinking away a tear of happiness. The Sherlock Holmes of yesteryear was back.

After only one pipe, Holmes pointed at my Indian Army uniform. He shot me an unexpected question. "Watson, I presume sun-up would have had a vital role in your Regiment's confrontation with Ayub Khan at the Battle of Maiwand. Isn't that where you received an arrow in your right leg?"

"Left shoulder," I replied. "And it was a Jezail long-arm rifle bullet, not an arrow."

"My point is, Watson, did you become something of an expert on the daily motion of the sun?"

"I had to – and did," I responded.

"To the point you can calculate the very moment of sunrise?"

"Yes, Holmes, but it's far from as simple as you might think. First, you must decide upon your definition of sunrise – is it when the middle of the sun crosses the horizon, or the top edge, or the bottom edge? Also, do you take the horizon to be sea level, or do you take into account the topography? In addition, what of the Earth's atmosphere? It can bend the light so the sun appears to rise a few moments earlier or later than if there were no atmosphere."

Holmes's expression turned from one of interest to irritation. He tore the briar from his mouth. "Yes, Watson, yes," he flared. "I consider the brain to be like an empty attic. We must stock it with just such furniture as we choose. Next you'll be telling me the Earth goes around the sun! I merely want to know whether – if given a while with a notebook and pencil – you can calculate the exact time this photograph was taken?"

I replied, "If we say sunrise refers to the time the middle of the disc of the sun appears on the horizon, considered unobstructed relative to the location of interest, and assuming atmospheric conditions to be average, and being sure to include the sun's declination from the time of the year..."

"Yes, yes, yes!" Holmes bellowed. "Take all of that into account, by all means!"

A telephone call from Holmes's bee-farm ensured we were greeted at the Museum's imposing entrance by Sir Frederick Kenyon, the Director. Sir Frederick was a palaeographer and biblical and classical scholar of the Old School. Our host led us to a small antechamber. The first drawer he opened revealed a glittering array of gold hoops and gold rivets, several silver collars and neck-rings, a silver arm, a fragment of a Permian ring, and a silver penannular brooch. Each was meticulously labelled. Sir Frederick picked out a sword pommel. "Mediaeval battles," he announced. "This was Lacey's life's work – the Battle of Fulford, the Siege of Exeter. Never have I had a colleague who worked with such application. For years at a time, he would hardly leave to go home at night – that is, until..." He paused.

"Until?" I echoed.

Sir Frederick looked at Holmes. "I don't know how else to put it – until Mr. Holmes failed to come to his help in finding the missing artefacts."

A flush of colour sprang to Holmes's pale cheeks.

I interjected quickly, "Was it also from this drawer that the items of no intrinsic value were disappearing?"

The Director shook his head.

"Not from here, no." He pulled open a second drawer. "From here."

The drawer was empty except for an envelope. It contained the letter I penned years earlier to the former Keeper of Antiquities, apologising for Holmes's refusal to become involved in the investigation. I had reconstructed Holmes's own words to read '*Mr. Sherlock Holmes sends his regrets. He is attending to his bee-farm in the South Downs and will not be taking cases for the foreseeable future.'*

"The missing artefacts were kept in this drawer," Sir Frederick continued, "where Lacey kept the more common or garden pieces found at various battle-sites. Broken sword-blades, horse-bits and the like. Miscellany too lacking in value or utility even for the local peasantry to pick up. Nevertheless he took the theft very hard."

Sir Frederick looked sympathetically at my companion. "Mr. Holmes, I understand your refusal. There wasn't a gold or silver item or precious jewel among the lot." Our host hesitated, then added, "Despite this, Lacey did seem unusually affected by Dr. Watson's letter. His behaviour changed. He grew secretive. Now I reflect on it, it was as though he was developing a *plan*."

Sir Frederick continued, "I noticed one other change. Other people's fame began to obsess him. For example, when the antiquarian Charles Dawson declared the human-like skull he had uncovered near Piltdown to be the 'missing link' between ape and man, Lacey muttered something about making a discovery one day which would make his own name just as famous – not in anthropology but in the annals of English archaeology."

I asked, "Do you have any idea what he meant?"

The Museum Director shrugged. "One day I came in upon him unexpectedly. He was bent over that table studying a drawing. Beyond saying it involved electrical theory, he would elaborate no further."

"Electrical theory?" I heard Holmes echo, asking, "Do you recall anything from the drawing itself?"

The Director shook his head. "I chanced only a quick glance before Lacey slipped it under some other papers. There were wires. I spotted a few words in French. I remember there were two large wheels, one at each end of the legs of a bipod. Oh yes, something about the wheels was odd. They weren't upright like a dogcart or other means of conveyance. They were flat on the ground."

"What were the words in French?" I asked.

"'*Faisceau hertzien*'," came the reply. "I'm told that means *wireless beam*. My curiosity overcame me. "Lacey," I said, "I'd be grateful if you kindly let me in on this secret of yours!" But all he muttered was something about unexploded bombs. Then he got up from the table and said he'd been meaning to talk to me. About retirement. He said if Europe's greatest Consulting Detective couldn't be bothered to look into the theft of artefacts from the British Museum, his faith in human beings was gone. A month or so later, he handed in his resignation and quit."

The great doors of the Museum shut behind us. I hailed a motorised hackney. "Waste of time coming all the way here, wasn't it, Holmes!" I remarked, "I can't say we learnt much about anything."

Holmes's eyebrows arched. "On the contrary, Watson, I think we learnt a very great deal. Take Lacey's violent reaction when he received your letter. Even to hand in his resignation! I'd have expected him to be exercised if the priceless gold and jewelled artefacts had been filched. None of those went missing despite being right next to the drawer containing quite ordinary relics. You'd have thought even the most common or garden sneak thief in something of a hurry can spot the difference between a gold torque and a rusty link from a dead Saxon's chain-mail armour."

The cab circled back in response to my wave and came to a halt at the kerb in front of us. Once seated, Holmes continued musing. "Why would the loss of a few worthless battlefield gew-gaws generate such a clamour from the Keeper?"

"Monomania perhaps?" I answered. "As you know, there's a term the French novelist Honoré de Balzac invented, '*idée fixe*', describing how one particular obsession may still be accompanied in every other way by complete sanity."

Holmes asked, "What do you make of the other curious matter, the machine depicted in the blueprint? A bipod with two large wheels flat against the ground?"

"I haven't the faintest idea, Holmes, nor why the subject of unexploded bombs would come up at the British Museum."

"True," Holmes responded thoughtfully. "It's certainly an odd subject for a Keeper of Antiquities."

We arrived at Victoria Station. The train trundled over the Thames. The last low rays of the setting sun sparkled against the cross atop the great dome of St Paul's Cathedral. We were on our way back to Sussex.

After a lengthy walk in Holmes's woods and fields that evening, we returned to the farmhouse. I struck a match on my boot and put it to the fire laid earlier by Mrs. Keppler to ward off the country damp. The ancient hearth blazed up as heartily as in our days at 221B, Baker Street, fuelled from the abundant oak, so abundant it was known as 'the Weed of Sussex', rather than the sea-coal in our London fireplace. I opened my notebook and said, "Holmes, you asked where the sun was at the instant the camera shutter was released. Judging by the shadows, I believe the photograph was taken when the geometric centre of the rising sun was eighteen degrees below low hills to the south-east. Around 6.40 a.m. That was the first moment there would have been enough light."

My companion absorbed this in silence. A few minutes later he asked in a solicitous tone, "If Captain Watson of the Army Medical Department were to consult Dr. John H. Watson, M.D. at the latter's renowned medical practice in Marylebone, would Dr. Watson tell the Captain he has fully recovered from a frightful ordeal in Mesopotamia, followed by incarceration in a Turkish dungeon?"

"Thank you, Holmes," I replied, touched by this rare concern. "You may take it the Captain's heart would be certified as strong as that of the proverbial ox. Daily walks on the warship returning Captain Watson to these shores, combined with the fine food of the Naval Officer's Mess, completely restored him."

"Excellent!" my companion exclaimed, a trifle enigmatically. He leaned with his back against the shutters, the deep-set grey eyes narrowing. "Watson, we hold in our hand the threads of one of the strangest cases ever to perplex a man's brain, yet we lack the one or two clues which are needful to complete a theory of mine. Ah, I see you yawning. I suggest you retire. I shall tarry over a pipe a while longer to see if light can be cast on our path ahead."

The country air and the warmth of the log-fire had taken their effect. I hadn't the slightest idea what Holmes was up to or whether or how the strength of "Captain Watson's" heart could have anything to do with the present perplexing case. I fell into a comfortable bed and a restful sleep.

I was dreaming of I know not what when a loud rat-tat-tat came on the bedroom door. "Watson!" Holmes called out. "We must throw our brains into action. Dress quickly!" I opened an eye. Through the window, Venus and Mars were in close conjunction, bright in an otherwise cloudy night sky. "What is it, Holmes?" I returned indignantly. "Can't it wait till dawn?"

The door flew open. My impatient host entered, dressed for the outdoors in Norfolk jacket and knickerbockers, with a cloth cap upon his head. "*Genii locorum.* As you know, I'm a believer in visiting the scene of the crime. It is essential in the proper exercise of deduction to take the perspective of those involved. I have just returned from Battle. I must return there with you straight away. Just one thread remains, my dear fellow. You are the one person who can provide it."

Scarcely an hour later, Holmes and I stood side by side on the spot where William the Conqueror's knights crushed King Harold's housecarls and his Saxon freemen. Holmes flapped a hand over a patch of grass. "I estimate the corpse lay here. Watson. How long before the geometric centre of the rising sun reaches eighteen degrees below the horizon?"

I looked to the south-east. "Not more than five minutes," I replied, adding, "May I say I'm at a complete loss to know what in heaven's name we're doing here, Holmes. The dawn hasn't even…"

"Then Watson, you must have your answer!" Holmes shouted. "TURN TO FACE THE ABBEY!"

I whirled around. A terrifying apparition burst upon my startled gaze. With no sound audible above my stentorian breathing, a knight in chainmail astride a huge charger was flying down the slope towards me, a boar image on his helmet, on an arm a kite shield limned with a Crusader cross and six *Fleur De Lis*. Behind, half-a-dozen cowled monks rose out of the ground, menacing, crouching, uttering strange cries. I broke into a cold, clammy sweat. My muscles twitched uncontrollably. I felt I was about to crash to the ground. The immense horse and rider passed by in a split second, dashing on until the pair merged with the spectral mist rising from a clump of bushes a hundred yards down the slope. I turned to face the ghostly monks. There was no one there. It was as though a preternatural visitation had returned to the Netherworld with the first shafts of the rising sun.

I had fallen to all fours, dazed. Holmes's voice came to me faintly, as though from a distant shore. "Watson, my dear fellow, are you all right? You've had a terrible shock." The familiar voice brought me back to sanity.

“We can agree that I have, Holmes,” I panted, struggling to clear my head. In the same reassuring tone, Holmes went on, “The phantoms have gone, my dear friend. They’ve returned to their rest. They will not be back until the next anniversary of the Battle of Hastings.”

I looked around the empty sward. “Where on Earth…?” I began.

“Tunnels, my dear fellow,” Holmes answered. “Monks and other ecclesiasticals. Landed Gentry. Knights Templar. Abbots. All particularly given to tunnels.”

The terror I endured for those few seconds was dissipating. Holmes looked at me closely. “Again I ask, are you all right, my dear fellow?”

“I am nearly recovered,” I said. “I appreciate your evident concern, Holmes, but you are clearly not an innocent party to this strange event. I deserve and demand an explanation.”

Holmes seated himself on the ground at my side. “Two clues put me on a scent. First, the trace evidence around us here.” His finger described an ellipse following the trajectory of the ghostly horse as it galloped down to the swamp. “Look there, and there,” he ordered.

I stared at the series of depressions in the grass. “But Holmes,” I protested, “while those indentations may fit where a horse’s hooves would have landed, they are both too shallow and too square for the marks of a horse ridden at speed!”

“My dear Captain Watson, do I take it even in your service in the Far East you failed to hear of mediaeval Japanese straw horse-sandals known as *umugatsu*? They were tied between the fetlock and hoof to give traction on wet terrain and to muffle the sound of the hooves, and to deceive by eliminating the deep cuts hooves would inflict on damp earth. I think we can credit the local schoolmaster for his scholarship.”

"Nice touch. The Crusader shield too," I remarked sarcastically, "when you consider the first Crusade didn't commence until thirty years after the Battle of Hastings."

I fingered my pulse. It was returning to normal. "And the second of two clues, Holmes?"

"The second lay in the difference between the print I purchased and the same photograph as it appeared in *The Battle Observer*. The editor wanted only the corpse's face and the arrow. Therefore, Hanson enlarged the middle of the print. This brought out a granulated effect in the grass under the head. But why? Why was there any graininess about the background at all? Why weren't the blades of grass as much in focus as the face and arrow?"

"Holmes," I responded, "Since you brought the matter up yesterday I have given it some thought. Forgive me if what I'm about to propose sounds absurd, but I'm very far from being unacquainted with cameras, as you know. The only explanation is the camera must have been positioned much higher up than if held by someone standing on the ground in the normal way. Getting the face in precise focus at the greater distance would mean anything deeper would be less in focus. This effect would show up most when the photograph was enlarged."

"The very conclusion I came to myself, Watson!" my companion exclaimed, rubbing his hands in delight. The *occipitofrontalis* muscles of my forehead wrinkled. I asked, "But why would Hanson stretch his arms high over his head to take the photo?"

"He wouldn't," came the response. "He didn't need to. He was seated on a horse. The knight was none other than *The Observer* photographer himself."

I waved at the field stretching away above us. "Holmes, how in Heaven's name did you get them to cooperate?"

“Not eight hours ago, I paid Hanson a visit,” Holmes replied. “He admitted everything. I told him he and his co-conspirators could be in mortal danger. Frightening someone to death could be murder, and that my silence was not safeguard enough – others may yet make the same deduction. He said “I’m the one who thought up the caper. If anyone is to meet the hangman, it should be me.”

I told him I had something in mind. He and the monks were to reassemble here before dawn today.” Holmes tapped his watch and raised and dropped an arm. “At my signal, the knight was to charge straight at the man in a captain’s uniform at my side. The monks were once again to spring up like dragon’s teeth, yelling any doggerel they could remember from schoolboy Latin.”

The explanation jolted me to the core. “Holmes!” I yelled. I broke off, breathing hard. “Holmes,” I repeated, “I once described you as a brain without a heart, as deficient in human sympathy as you are pre-eminent in intelligence. Are you proving me right? Are you saying that despite Lacey’s frightful death, you deliberately exposed me to an identical fate?”

“Yes, my dear Captain,” Holmes broke in, chuckling, “I did. You must remember I took the precaution of checking on your health with a Dr. Watson, famed on two continents for his medical skills. He pronounced your heart strong as an ox. Who am I to dispute his diagnosis?”

“And if the good Dr. Watson had made a misjudgement?” I asked ruefully.

“High stakes indeed, Watson,” came the rejoinder. “I would have lost a great friend, and a hapless crew of locals their best witness, leaving me bereft and them open to a second charge of murder! But you survived, therefore it can be claimed Lacey’s heart was already weakened in the extreme.”

My legs still felt shaky. "Holmes," I begged. "Why are you so adamantly on these people's side?"

"Think of this small town, Watson," my comrade began. "Eight hundred and fifty years ago, when Duke William crossed the Channel there was no human settlement here, just a quiet stretch of rough grazing. Look at it now! Without the battlefield, it would be nothing, a backwater, a small and isolated market-town. Imagine Royal Windsor without the Castle, Canterbury without the Cathedral. Visitors to this battleground provide the underpinning of every merchant on the High Street, the hoteliers and publicans, even *The Battle Observer* itself, dependent on advertising Philpott's Annual Summer Sales and the like. The mock monks and a spectral knight on horseback can fairly be accused of one thing – trying to protect their livelihoods. If visitors stop coming, the hotels die. The souvenir shops die. The cafés and restaurants close.

"Napoleon greatly incensed the English by calling us 'a nation of shopkeepers', and England remains a nation of merchants. All her grand resources arise from commerce. What else constitutes the riches of England? It's not mines of gold, silver, or diamonds. Not even extent of territory. We are a tiny island off the great landmass of Eurasia."

Holmes pointed to where ghostly horse and rider had disappeared. "Have you recovered enough to walk down to that clump of bushes? I anticipate we shall find something there of extreme interest."

At the bottom of the slope, a small bridge took us to a speckle of marshland dotted about with bushes and reeds into which horse and rider had disappeared. Holmes's former quick pace slowed like the Clouded Leopard searching out its prey. With a grunt of satisfaction, he darted forward, calling out "Come, Watson – give me a hand!" A pair of wooden spars jutted from the mud. A spade half-floated on the mud a few feet beyond.

We dragged the contraption to dry ground. It was the physical embodiment of the blueprint the Keeper of Antiquities had tried to hide at the British Museum. Held upright, the bipod was perhaps three feet in height. It was exactly as described by Sir Frederick. The two wheels were not the wheels of a small cart but circles of wood and metal lying flush with the ground, some twenty-four inches apart. A set of wires led to a half-submerged metal box filled with vacuum tubes and a heavy battery.

I pointed. "Holmes, those are Audion vacuum tubes. I've seen them used in wireless technology. This must be the secret invention Lacey hinted at."

"If he had not built it, Watson," Holmes responded, "Lacey might still be alive." He continued, "I pondered long and hard about '*Faisceau hertzien*', and the reference to unexploded bombs. Then by chance, my brother Mycroft called to say he had been seconded to the War Office for the duration. In the greatest confidence, he told me the French 6th Engineer Regiment at Verdun-sur-Meuse has been developing a machine using wireless beams to detect German mines. Somehow Lacey must have heard about it. He realised he could adapt it to search for metal artefacts at ancient battlegrounds."

"But, Holmes," I asked. "Why use it on this field? After all, if Lacey's intention was to *disprove* the battle took place here…"

"It was Lacey's '*idée fixe*'," my companion interrupted.

He pointed at the spade. "He criss-crossed these fields at night using a device which could spot even a silver penny dropped nine centuries ago. With it, he was able to detect and remove every metal artefact left by Duke William's and King Harold's men. However, Lacey may have found nothing whatsoever, not even a piece of rusty chainmail, thereby proving the battle never took place here. On the other hand, possibly he was clearing it of anything traceable to 1066 – in short, planning a great evil against the noble profession of Archaeology. Either way, at a moment of maximum publicity on the anniversary, he intended to denounce the town's claim to the battle-site. He did not give a thought that the town's prosperity would come to an abrupt end. Then one recent moonlit night, the photographer Brian Hanson saw this phantom-like figure moving slowly across the landscape. He recognised Lacey. He guessed what he was up to. The townsfolk had to work fast. They set about enacting the show of mediaeval knights and monks they had been practicing for months."

I looked back up the slope.

"Inducing stress cardiomyopathy," I murmured. "Should we go to report our findings to the local police?"

"By no means," came a firm reply.

I turned to stare at my companion. "But… but surely, now we know?"

"Watson, we need do nothing but wait to see if the matter progresses or simply dies away. Remember, the local Police knew of my presence in the region but failed to enlist my help. At the very least, if charges *are* brought, thanks to your evidence no jury of twelve good men and true will convict for murder."

"How should that be, Holmes?" I asked, "when indisputably their actions caused the death of a man. How can they escape the hangman's noose?"

"Because our motley crew of locals didn't have murder in mind. They rose up out of the ground dressed as the disquieted souls of long-dead Benedictine monks. Their plan was simply to frighten him off and fling his infernal contrivance and spade into the swamp. That that was their intent is the more credible, thanks to your survival. They now have a good case to plead *Mens rea* – no mental intent to kill. At worst manslaughter, not murder."

"The arrow?" I asked.

"Admittedly a barbarous act," Holmes replied, "but the man was already dead. Hanson hoped to confuse the coroner, to make him conclude the arrow caused the stricken expression on the corpse's face and was self-inflicted. Suicide. Otherwise, alarm bells would ring, and a case for murder arise."

I asked, "And who would want to associate the vile crime of murder with these dear old homesteads set in a smiling and beautiful countryside? Another case resolved, Holmes. Let us leave the good people of Battle to their commemorative preparations and repair to our favourite eatery deep among the Downs – in short, a visit to the Tiger Inn to partake of a hearty lunch."

We heaved the spade deeper into the marsh and marked the unexploded-bomb detector's location for retrieval by Mycroft Holmes's agents at a later time. As we walked back across the small bridge, I said, "There's a matter you have not explained. Why did the Keeper of Antiquities react in such a choleric way to your refusal to investigate?"

"It was a ruse quite worthy of arch-criminal Moriarty of old, Watson, a most devious ploy. A snub was precisely what Lacey wanted. We should have smelt a rat by the way he worded his request – '*I shall of course understand if this case is of little interest to you, Mr. Holmes, the missing articles being of no intrinsic value whatsoever*'. That's hardly as compelling as '*Mr. Holmes, while the relics are of scant intrinsic value, from the historical point of view they are very nearly unique*'. Your letter informing him of my refusal came to him like Manna from Heaven. He could show Sir Frederick he'd tried to bring in Europe's most famous Consulting Detective. No one would ever dream the larcenist was Lacey himself. He would be able to use the pilfered artefacts to 'salt' the field of his choosing, at nearby Netherfield, for example."

"Thereby," I added, "becoming one of the most famous men in England."

"Yes," my companion nodded. "As famous in the archaeological world as Charles Dawson in the world of the palaeontologist and anatomist."

Together we walked across the historic fields. A line of horse-drawn cabs was forming at the Abbey entrance, the fine arrangement of bays and cobs ready for the day's great influx of visitors, snorting into their nosebags. We went over to a Landau driven by a pair.

"Cabbie, the Tiger Inn," Holmes instructed. "A military guinea for you from the captain here if we arrive before their kitchen runs out of that well-armed sea creature, the Cornish lobster."

NOTE

Footnote 1. '*I stared up at the patch of blue sky visible through a tiny grille high up on the wall. I was a prisoner-of-war in Constantinople, left to rot in a dank cell under the magnificent State rooms of Sultan Mehmed V Reşâd's Palace…*'
As Watson notes, 10 years beforehand, an earlier Sultan, Abd-ul-Hamid II, had received Sherlock Holmes and him in that same Palace as honoured guests. The case was published under the title 'Sherlock Holmes and the Sword of Osman'.

Joseph Conrad's '*The Secret Agent*'. Watson had Conrad's novel to hand in his stint in the dungeon under the Dolmabahçe Palace, Constantinople. The terrorism and anarchism in the plot fitted well into the paranoia of the years leading up to the First World War. *The Independent* called it one of Conrad's great city novels, and the *New York Times* described it as '*the most brilliant novelistic study of terrorism*'.

Trichinopoly cigar. The Trichie was a major Indian export in British Victorian times, a cheap cheroot that the town of Trichy or Triruchirappalli in Tamil Nadu, India, is famous for. Trichinopoly was the name of the town in British times. The cigar-makers fermented the tobacco for a few years in distilled fruit juice (pineapple, grape, orange, apple) with added honey and jaggery (made of the products of sugarcane and the toddy palm tree). It's joked that an attachment for the Tritchie was one thing Sherlock Holmes and Winston Churchill had in common.

Genii locorum. In classical Roman religion, the protective spirits of a place.

A military guinea. The name 'Military' Guinea comes from the fact it was minted to pay the armed forces in the Napoleonic wars rather than less-acceptable paper money. Only around 80,000 of these coins were struck, making them a rare collectors item today.

The Battle of Hastings. Watson says, "*Another case resolved, Holmes. Let us leave the good people of Battle to their commemorative preparations*", but it should be noted the exact site of a battle which changed world history has never been definitively settled. In 2013 even a professional team of archaeologists with metal detectors and considerable experience of uncovering ancient settlements found absolutely no artefacts, let alone the plethora of broken bits of metal, smashed skulls and other accoutrements one would expect from such a savage battle a thousand years ago. The real site may still be 'out there', within a few miles and waiting to be discovered.

The Case Of The Seventeenth Monk

Chapter I

A Visitor Arrives at Watson's Clinic

Spring 1914. The Whittington chimes of the grandfather clock flooded along the hallway. It was five o'clock. I was alone in the consulting room of my medical practice in London's fashionable Marylebone district. If no further patients came, I could soon stroll to the In and Out Naval and Military Club for Soup of the Day and Whitebait. I crossed to the window and stared out. A light drizzle put me into a contemplative mood. My old friend Sherlock Holmes and I were no longer lodgers together at 221B, Baker Street. Some months had passed since he retired at the very height of his powers, to the relief of the criminal underworld. The decision had taken me utterly by surprise. Up to then I thought I had become an institution around Holmes, like his Stradivarius, or the old, oily black clay pipe, or his index books. Was it possible recent cases like 'The Creeping Man' would be the last exploits on which we would work together? Would we never again be crammed into an agile hansom rattling towards Charing Cross Station, my service revolver tucked into a pocket?

The thread which united many of the cases was the manner in which they began life. Francis Bacon tells us, "*If the mountain will not come to Muhammad, then Muhammad must go to the mountain*". Before Holmes retired to his bee-farm in Sussex, it could be said he was that proverbial mountain. The case I published as '*A Study In Scarlet'* established his credentials as England's premier unofficial Consulting Detective, praised by no less a pair of Scotland Yard inspectors than Gregson and Lestrade. From then on there was no need for Holmes to advertise in *The Police Gazette* nor ingratiate himself with the well-to-do to obtain custom. His new-found *droit d'entrée* extended even to the highest reaches of European Society. The stairs at our lodgings once took the weight of the giant Wilhelm Gottsreich Sigismond von Ormstein, Grand Duke of Cassel-Felstein and King of Bohemia. The King was desperate to regain possession of a photograph taken with a certain "well-known adventuress", Irene Adler. The curious case of '*The Red-Headed League*' commenced when a flame-haired pawnbroker by the name of Jabez Wilson climbed those same stairs.

Holmes's career spawned as many want-to-be-Holmeses as Scotland's turbulent geology had spawned the Munros. Portraits of Holmes in watercolour, wood, and poker-work proliferated. Everywhere, men (and at least one woman) dressed in long grey travelling cloaks and deerstalker caps, old briar-root pipes *à la bouche*, expounding on the characteristics of different tobacco-ash (typically flakes of Latakia tobacco), poisons, stains, handwriting, and even the classification of mud and soil.

I returned to my desk. My eyes fixed themselves upon the framed picture of General 'Chinese' Gordon. What had he felt, holding Khartoum against the overwhelming Mahdi forces for more than a year? My train of thought was broken at exactly five minutes to six o'clock by a tap of finger-nails on the mahogany door of the consulting room. It heralded the entry of the receptionist, Miss Campbell, to announce her departure for home. "No more patients, Doctor," she said, drawing on her winter coat, "but there's someone in the waiting room who would like a word. Seems to be acquainted with you."

It was Miss Campbell's habit to provide me with a brief description of my patients prior to bringing them into the room. Over the months these descriptions had grown more and more adventurous and even clinical. At the start of her engagement, she merely gave name and age. Now I might be given a fully-fledged diagnosis with a suggested remedy, as in a case the previous week involving the mistress of the illustrious Lord --------, who came complaining of faintness and indigestion. "You should tell her not to lace her corsets so tightly," Miss Campbell advised, "and anyway, the small-corseted waist is falling out of fashion."

"He or she?" I asked, referring to the latest visitor.

"He."

"Did he give a name?" I asked.

"No," came the reply.

"Description?"

"Corpulent."

"Corpulent?" I repeated.

"Gargantuan, in fact."

"Gargantuan!" I parroted. I knew only one person for whom that description was invested with such meaning.

"Surely it can't be…" I began, getting to my feet.

"Indeed it is, Doctor," a voice interrupted from the corridor, "but I'd rather remain anonymous." He moved into the room. "Shall we say, 'Mr. Smith'?" he requested.

With a practiced move, his large hands took Miss Campbell by the shoulders and eased her out of the room, pushing the heavy door shut behind her.

I moved forward quickly. "My Heavens, Mycroft, this is a surprise!" I exclaimed, extending my hand. I looked up at the steel-grey, deep-set eyes and masterful brow of Sherlock Holmes's brother, the elder by some seven years. "And very welcome, of course!" I added. I pointed to the walnut Open Armchair. "Please," I continued, "do have a seat."

I had last come across Mycroft Holmes a year or so ago on a brief visit to the Diogenes, the unusual club he co-founded specifically for the most unsociable and unclubbable men in town where, save in the Stranger's

Room, no talking is under any circumstances allowed. Mycroft operated in some indeterminate fashion at the very heart of Government. During the case I titled '*The Bruce-Partington Plans'*, Sherlock Holmes said of his brother, "Occasionally he *is* the British government, the most indispensable man in the country…he is the central exchange, the clearinghouse, which makes out the balance. All other men are specialists, but his specialism is omniscience."

Holmes went on, "If the art of the detective began and ended in reasoning from an arm-chair, my brother would be the greatest criminal agent that ever lived. But he has no ambition and no energy. He will not even go out of his way to verify his own solution, and would rather be considered wrong than take the trouble to prove himself right."

I went to the door and called out loudly, "Miss Campbell, before you take your hat, please bring a fresh pot of tea."

I looked back at my guest.

"Any preference?" I asked.

"Gyokuro would be very welcome," he replied.

"Gyokuro," I relayed along the corridor. "And pastries and Devonshire cream, please!"

My visitor settled his vast bulk into the chair. He looked at me thoughtfully. A silence ensued. It's true, I thought. There *was* a suggestion of uncouth physical inertia about him.

Then, "Have you heard anything from Sherlock recently?" he asked.

"Not recently, no," I replied.

"Over the past month, say?"

I shook my head. "I rarely hear from him. Your brother retired to his bee-farm. Even before, he never made a habit of informing me of his every move."

Mycroft Holmes pointed at the telephone on my desk. "No telephone calls? Not even a telegram?"

I shook my head. "No contact from any quarter," I replied. "I assumed his wretched bees have been keeping him busy. But tell me, why of all people asking, if there's anyone in this world who would be *au fait* with his…"

"Exactly," came the reply.

Conversation was suspended while the tray of tea and pastries was brought in and distributed. The door shut once more.

Mycroft Holmes resumed, "You see, two months ago my brother was temporarily persuaded to come out of retirement. This was at the express instance of the Foreign Secretary, the Most Honourable Marquess of Lansdowne. For a very important mission. We impressed on Sherlock that the fate of our Empire might be at stake."

"The fate of our Empire?" I exclaimed. "And you are here in my surgery because…?"

"…We need to find out what's happened."

"How do you mean, 'find out what's happened'?"

"For example, if he's still alive."

I stared at my visitor.

"I'm sorry to sound like a parrot, Mycroft, but why would he not be alive?" I spluttered.

Mycroft Holmes pointed to the day-book on my desk.

"The question is, can you take a few weeks off to go *incognito* and look for him? Your knowledge of his ways might be invaluable."

"I can always bring in a *locum* from St. Mary's," I replied.

My guest set the cup down and pulled his great bulk up from the divan.

"I take that as a yes?" he asked.

I nodded. Watching him rise, I asked, "Surely you're going to give me a few instructions?"

"Only that you must take your service revolver and a box of ammunition. As to how you'll get there, we'll arrange that. Best not to go with Thomas Cook's."

"Am I allowed to know just a little more precisely where I'm going and what I'm meant to do when I get there?"

"You'll be going to Sherlock's last-known location. There's a German we asked him to keep watch upon, someone whose movements have been reported to the Foreign Secretary. Our Defence Attaché in Berlin rates the man *facile princeps* among the secret agents of the Kaiser."

"And his name?" I asked.

"Otto Müller, though he won't be using his real name, any more than Sherlock has been using his or you will yours. We've been aware of Müller for some time. As a young lieutenant, he was commissioned by the Kaiser to lead an expedition into uncharted territories of Central Asia, hand-picked for his unscrupulous nature. The group traversed vast plains and high, rugged mountains. They underwent the widest daily temperature ranges on Earth and suffered extraordinary privations. Müller was the only one to get back alive. We need to know what he's up to now. If he'd been living here, I would rate him the most dangerous man in England. Cross him and your life is not worth a pfennig, as Sherlock may have found out. If you come across him, under no circumstance – and I repeat – *under no circumstances* are you to directly approach him. Is that clear, Doctor? We simply want to know why he's there."

"Where are we talking about?" I asked.

"An impoverished island in the Mediterranean – two-thirds of it sterile rock."

"Why is the Kaiser taking such an interest in the place?"

"That's our question too."

"If it's so impoverished," I rejoined, "why would we care?"

"Because it straddles the sea lanes connecting England to our Empire in the East. Unlike other Empires – Russia, Germany, the Qing, the Ottoman – ours is a thalassocracy. We may rule vast areas of land and command further great stretches, but England's security lies in sovereignty of the seas. Britannia protects, manages, and controls oceans. Nothing must be allowed to threaten England's *Cordon Sanitaire* around our India possessions. The island in question is not isolated in a waste of waters. If the Kaiser gains mastery over it and war were to break out between Germany and Great Britain…"

For a last moment Mycroft Holmes stood in the doorway, his frame completely filling it.

"I envy you the journey to the lands and seas of Perseus, Jason and the Argonauts, Heracles, and Theseus. You must visit ancient Itanos, the city famed in antiquity as the gift of Mark Anthony to Cleopatra. As to who *you* are," he continued, "don't adopt a *ruse de guerre* such as a former riverboat captain on the Congo. There's always someone around likely to catch you out. Remain a medical man, but *not* by the name of Dr. John H. Watson. Was there another Assistant Surgeon with the 66th Foot at the Battle of Maiwand. For example, someone who attended you when you fell victim to the Afghan musket? You could use his name."

Any reminder of the heroism and incompetence of that fateful battle caused me to shudder even those many years later. It was a British trait to make legend out of abject military failure – the retreat to Corunna, the Charge of the Light Brigade, General Gordon's tragic death at Khartoum. At Maiwand, the 66th were not even aware of a ravine to our right. The Ghazi warriors used this cover to attack. We were exposed for three hours to the most horrific artillery fire an army ever had to stand, all concentrated from the front and flanks on a small surface not two-hundred yards long. Finally the order came to up-and-run, or in my case to be hauled away bleeding by my brave orderly Murray.

"There was an Army Surgeon with me at Maiwand," I replied. "A British Captain. I last heard he was in South Africa."

"Even better. He won't be around to contradict your theft of his name. For the rest, you can stay close to the truth. You were badly wounded and discharged with an Army pension, and you are developing an interest in archaeology."

"And the name of this poverty-stricken little place?" I asked.

"Not so little. It's some one hundred and sixty miles from north to south and thirty five miles at its broadest. The classic Land of Minôs – the Isle of Crete."

Holmes's brother chose to exit by the Tradesman's Entrance. Outside we shook hands. "Curious story, the Cretan Minotaur," he said. "Dante mentions him in the *Inferno*." In a warning tone he added, "Doctor, Crete is and has always been a land where death trumps life. It's possible my brother's bones lie there now. Take care yours don't get left there too."

He turned, climbed into a large Lanchester Tonneau, and was gone.

I went upstairs into an attic where I kept the battered old trunk from my military days. I knew little of Crete other than its location in the Eastern Mediterranean, its topography ribbed by bare, almost treeless mountains, a link between Asia, Africa, and Europe. I took out a map last used aboard the troopship *HMS Orontes*, sailing through the Mediterranean on my return to England, pensioned off with eleven shillings and six pence a day. I put my trusty service revolver on the side to oil up later. Moths had done their work on the tropical wear in the tin box. While uncertain that I would be in Crete long enough for the boiling summer to reach its apogee, I would nevertheless pay a visit to Marshall and Snelgrove's and order a replacement for my old suit of Sichuan paj.

Chapter II

Watson Prepares To Sail To The Aegean

Mycroft's visit left me in a state of considerable agitation. I'd assumed that his brother's silence was a consequence of absorption in a new life with his "little working gangs" of *Apis mellifera*, the domesticated European Honey Bee – or perhaps engrossed in writing his promised magnum opus, *The Whole Art of Detection*. Surely it was impossible he was dead? If so, when word arrived in England, *The London Times* and *The Manchester Guardian* would come rushing to update their obituaries. I reflected how the announcements in the newspapers and journals at the time of his retirement had given the impression the great detective's soul had already departed for the Otherworld. Ruefully, I myself felt this was almost true, to forsake his convenient lodgings and a busy life at Baker Street – at the heart of the world's greatest metropolis – for the isolation of a villa on the Sussex Downs and harsh winter winds blasting in from the English Channel. *The Police Gazette* regretted his decision as premature, terming it '*disagreeable to all enemies of crime*', and listing his accomplishments in the past tense – '*Born 1854, great-nephew of the French artist Émile Jean-Horace Vernet. Skilled violinist and learned in the Oriental art of baritsu. Interested in chemistry, he frequently dabbled with poisons and acids. According to his* amanuensis *Dr. John H. Watson, he was an excellent singlestick player, boxer, and swordsman.*'

There followed a list of some of Holmes's publications. 'On Secret Writings', 'Upon the Distinction between the Ashes of the Various Tobaccos', 'On the Typewriter and Its Relation to Crime', 'Upon the Tracing of Footsteps' and 'Upon the Dating of Old Documents'. Through his knowledge of the types of tobacco ashes, he could, *The Gazette* noted, '*identify the kinds of cigarettes found at a crime scene*' and '*distinguish different types of shoe prints, footprints, horseshoe prints, and hound-dog prints*'.

The London Times noted Holmes was a master of disguises. '*With the ease of a great actor he became a bookseller, a groom, a clergyman, an old Italian priest, a seaman, a plumber, and even an old woman.*' *The Illustrated London News* remarked on Holmes's extraordinary facility with languages, '*as at ease with Middle Egyptian hieroglyphs as with Goethe's* 'Faust' *or Hugo's* 'Les Misérables'.'

The next morning, the twelve-horsepower twin-cylinder Lanchester Tonneau returned to the surgery. The chauffeur's traditional four-in-hand knot in his tie gave a pleasant nod to the long history of the horse-carriage he was helping sweep away. Willingly he provided an inspection of the vehicle's epicyclic gearbox and the ingenious balance of the horizontal engine, after which he handed over a package. It contained a *Laissez-Passer* in the name of Captain _______, M.D., plus a considerable sum in several currencies – English gold sovereigns, Ottoman gold *Kurush*, and Greek silver one- and two-*drachmae*. The receipt called for my signature as John H. Watson and not Captain _______. The oversight would probably ensure only hours would pass before the whole of the Foreign Office learned of my involvement.

The delivery was followed an hour later by the arrival of a letter bearing the insignia of the famous Manchester Ship Canal boatbuilders Abdela & Mitchell. The writing was distinguished by the ornamental style of the penmanship (the letter '*f*' upstroke twice the length of the downstroke, the upstroke for the shorter letter '*e*' two-thirds the vertical length of the downstroke).

I opened the letter. It read -

Dear Captain _______,

I understand you have accepted a position aboard a whaling ship and will be leaving for the Antarctic in four or five months' time. In the interim, I can offer you temporary employment. Our shipyard has completed trials of the Harouny, *a thirteen-ton launch destined for delivery via the French canals and Malta to a former Ottoman territory in the Eastern Mediterranean. Normally a surgeon would not be required, but there has been an outbreak of Mediterranean Fever along the route, occasioned by the* Micrococcus melitensis. *We therefore wonder if you might act as ship*'s *Medical Officer at a fee of two guineas a day plus all expenses? If so, you would need to be packed and ready at Manchester Dock 9 in two days' time.*

A response at your earliest convenience would be much appreciated.

I am,
Yrs very sincerely,

Isaac J. Abdela

I folded the letter and put it in my pocket. I would need supplies. I went to the telephone and placed an order with the Junior Navy Stores for a wicker luncheon basket to await my arrival at Dock 9. It would contain several packets of Fortnum's Royal Blend Tea ('*Notes of Flowery Pekoe from*

Ceylon uplifted with Maltier Assam'), twenty-five tins of ox tongues, five of pressed beef, thirty of turkey and tongue pâtés, four of ham, fifteen plum puddings, twelve guava jelly, and twenty-five tins of sardines and a dozen jars of Burgess's Genuine Anchovy Paste. From John Bell and Croyden I ordered ten bottles of Enos's Fruit Salts and a supply of quinine pills. A visit would also be required to tobacconists Salmon and Gluckstein of Oxford Street to purchase a half-dozen tins of J. and H. Wilson No. 1 Top Mill Snuff and several boxes of Trichinopoly cigars, manufactured from tobacco grown near the town of Dindigul.

After that, to Foyle's Bookshop at Cecil Court for a copy of William Clark Russell's latest nautical yarn, *Overdue*. Its five hundred and more adventurous pages would engage me aboard the *Harouny* through the roiling Bay of Biscay and the Alboran Sea and onward to my destination. By now a more optimistic mood had overtaken me. Would I once again be seated in a carriage or donkey-cart next to Holmes in distant Crete, revolver at the ready and the thrill of adventure in my heart?

I reached into a drawer and took out the time-piece lying there, a scratched champlevé green, blue-and-black enamel pocket-watch by Boget and Olivet, Geneve, in eighteen-karat gold. I would take it with me. It had a double sentimental value. Along with the nine-tube grandfather clock, it was the only object I had inherited from my father via my dead brother. Once in Baker Street, the pocket-watch had been a test I had given Holmes to gauge his deductive abilities. Holmes had passed with almost magical power.

The sea journey went without incident. I spent a nostalgic day at Malta's Grand Harbour where I had last stopped on my final journey back from Peshawar 35 years earlier. At dusk, silver bugles brought the notes of 'The

Setting of the Sun' on the breeze from *HMS Revenge* at anchor, followed from the *Harouny*'s engine-room with a rousing chorus of 'The Absent-Minded Beggar'.

That evening I lay on my comfortable bunk. My eyelids drooped and I checked my pocket-watch. It was still early. I tried to postpone sleep by reading aloud from Clark Russell's nautical yarn at a gripping point – "S*tand by all three royal halliards – mizzen top-gallant halliards" rapped out Captain Mostyn, in the quick harsh note of the sea command. "Helm there, let her go off two points*" – but without success. I put the book aside and prepared to give way to the pleasant lassitude.

Rather than dozing off, my mind leapt back to the most dramatic event in Sherlock Holmes's and my active years together, the fateful encounter at the Reichenbach Falls in the Swiss Alps between Holmes and the criminal mastermind Professor James Moriarty.

It was in April and May of 1891 that Holmes finally managed to outwit the Professor. On my comrade's instruction, the police had effected a series of arrests which cleaned up countless crimes and dismantled Moriarty's organisation. While this was taking place, Holmes and I prudently travelled to the Continent. It only later I realised my friend was using himself as bait to capture the Professor, who Holmes realised might well escape the Yard's net - and had.

Our journey led us by way of Meiringen to the Reichenbach Falls where I was duped away from Holmes, enabling my great friend to confront the Professor alone. The resulting clash of titans ended in Moriarty's death and the assumption of Holmes's own demise, as it was believed both had tumbled, locked together, into that dreadful cauldron. In fact, Holmes had escaped death, using his knowledge of Baritsu to topple his adversary into the raging torrent.

Many a criminal had underestimated Holmes. I wondered if I would find that to be the case in Crete, or whether this time Holmes had met his match.

I reached out and turned off the small side light.

Chapter III

The *Harouny* Reaches Crete

We lay off Crete. The *Harouny* had dropped anchor in the moonlight. A short while later, dawn broke over the town of Candia and we edged forward. Coasters were already at work loading bags of caoba from lighters. The horseshoe-shaped harbour was able to take only the tiniest steamers and sailing vessels. We had sailed from Valetta into the seas and lands of Homer, the mountains and coastlines alive with legendary figures – Achilles, Agamemnon, Helen and Menelaus, Odysseus, Penelope and Telemachus. I stood on the deck staring out at the wondrous scene before me, '*a land... in the midst of the wine-dark sea; fair, rich and sea-girt is she...*' Sea-girt, yes, but no longer rich, I thought. I gazed at the succession of tumbled-down, overgrown limestone walls of abandoned buildings. Ancient terraces ran wild with asphodels, marguerites, and rhododendrons. Beyond them rose a range of arid mountains. Was Holmes somewhere out there, lying dead, a fly-blown corpse awaiting the predation of *Gypaetus barbatus* – the Bearded Vulture? "How on Earth do I start the search?" I wondered out loud.

I received an answer the moment I stepped off the gang-plank. "Welcome to the land of King Minôs. My name," the man said with a bow, "is Stavraki Aristarchi." He wore white sheepskin boots and a costly alzarine silk sash about his waist. "I am a dragoman. I can be your guide." He turned his finger towards the *Harouny*'s jackstaff. "I speak excellent

English, but if you wish I can switch to German or French or Greek or Turkish or…"

"Hold on, Stavraki Aristarchi!" I chuckled, "English will be fine. First I need accommodation, and then we can discuss terms. I assume you'll be available for a fortnight or so?"

He would, he assured me, be available for the rest of my corporeal life if needed, and wished me a long and happy one.

A second figure approached. "*Effendi*," he asked, looking furtively this way and that, "can I interest you in an amethyst scarab? Twenty of your English pounds. From the Egyptian Twelfth Dynasty." He pointed towards the island's interior. "My nephew found it over there. In the Kamares Cave, very high on Mount Ida."

I decided to take the bull by the horns. I replied, "I'm not here to buy antiquities. I'm here to join up with an old friend and go to the Acropolis of Polirinnia, but I am not sure of his whereabouts."

"Go to the Acropolis of Polirinnia, you say?" the man asked, eyeing me carefully. "Your name, *Effendi*?"

"Captain _______," I replied. "I'm a Medical Doctor with an interest in archaeology."

"This friend, is he a Cretan like this dragoman, or a foreigner like you?"

I replied. "*Anglos*. Like me, except he is this tall…" (I indicated about six feet) "…and thinner, with deep-set grey eyes."

The souvenir seller studied me as an archaeologist would study a terracotta shard. "We know every foreigner who arrives and every foreigner who departs," he continued. "We count them in and we count them out." He held up the amethyst scarab. "They are important to us. We like the money they leave behind. There is a man like that…" Again he pointed southward. "...except I cannot vouch for the colour of his eyes."

"And this man?" I asked. "How would I find him?"

"If you travel as I tell you, you cannot miss him. He's offering ten silver *drachmae* for any pieces of burnt clay or pots with ancient *grammata* – writing – on them. He must be a spy. Who else would wear a dark cloak with a crimson lining? Who else but a spy would dress like that? Also because he wears square blue sunglasses," the man continued, "and because we think every foreigner is a spy. My friend here, the dragoman – maybe he's also a spy. He worked for the Ottoman pashas until we kicked them out. Maybe we should shoot him down like a dog! Maybe you too are a spy." He pointed at the *Harouny*. "All spies arrive on boats like that."

As casually as possible I asked, "Why would a spy bother to come here?"

"Because Crete is now free. Four hundred years under Imperial Butchers like İkinci Abdülhamit, the Turkish Sultan, are over. We worry we will become a pawn on some other chess-board. Even you British – wouldn't you like Crete to be another jewel in your King's crown?"

I reached into my pocket for an over-generous gratuity.

"Finding this *Effendi* would be a good start," I replied.

The vendor spoke to the dragoman. Looking dismayed, the dragoman muttered back to me. "The place he says, '*Einai stou diaolou ti mana*', translating immediately as '*It's at the devil's mother*' – is somewhere very hard to get to."

I reached out with the handful of one- and two-*drachmae* silver coins. The souvenir seller took them with a nod and turned to point into the distance. "Go to the sacred cave of the nymph Eileithyia. I sold the *Anglos* an old pot there a week ago. This man Stavraki Aristarchi can take you. I have two good mounts you can hire." He pointed at the considerable pile of luggage and tinned goods waiting to be lifted off the deck. “And a good mule you can hire too.”

We arranged to meet the mounts and mule in the town square early on the morrow. Pleased with our negotiations, the man departed with his scarab of dubious antiquity. I called after him, shouting above the harbour din, “And *your* name?”

“I was born on the island of the Aphrodite,” he shouted back. “You can call me Milos!”

The sun was rising from behind a headland on our right as we left Candia’s ramshackle agglomeration of dusty, friendly shops. I looked forward to the quiet of the countryside. It was ‘Little Easter’ and snails were being brought in in pailfuls. The rattle of cart-wheels along the descending main street had kept me awake all night. Milos had supplied two strong-boned Anadolu Ponies, along with a mule for my baggage. In thc cool of the morning, we clattered past a Venetian four-clog stone fountain before entering the long, dark tunnel of the Kainoriou Gate and crossing a narrow bridge over a Saracen moat. Two-wheeled one-mule carts, loose on their axles, rumbled past, the drivers asleep.

We overtook men on foot who seemed not at all to mind a load swinging between their legs like a bloated cow’s udder. Bread, cheese, olives – anything needed along the way – went into and swayed about in the capacious slack of their trousers. A ragged assembly of lepers let out for begging purposes from the nearby colony blocked our way, exhibiting their deformities in the hope of evoking concern and a few coins. I had seen victims of this terrible disease in the squalid districts of Bombay and Calcutta, the bacterium remorselessly spread by contact with fluid from the nose of an infected person. My dragoman scattered a handful of five-

lepta coins some yards to one side. The unfortunate creatures scrabbled in the dust for a share, opening up a passage for us.

Within the hour the roadside wine-shops died away. The dirt trail climbed through the remains of the sacred woods of Jupiter. Peasants astride wooden saddles on tiny donkeys passed us on their way to tend scattered stretches of ancient olives whose fruit may once have been gathered by Minoan hands. At around seven o'clock, we passed within earshot of Knossos. A roar of blasting powder told us the archaeologists were already hard at work.

Onward we travelled through valleys scattered with bright red anemones and spurge and yellow sage, and then up through mountain passes overgrown with oregano and rosemary, a herbalist's pharmacopoeia. The mixed perfumes rose like a bewitchment from the strike of our conveyances' hooves. For several hot and stony miles, we followed on a track which rose and fell. At midday we tied our rides and mule to the trees at the route's edge and walked out across a ridge to a knoll brilliant with purple, white, and pinkish anemones and blue irises. We lunched on guava jelly and tins of pressed beef, warmed by a fire kindled from chunks of gnarled brushwood lying all around. "We shall stop there for tonight, at 'The Aphrodite'," Stavraki Aristarchi informed me. He was pointing towards a lone limewashed building in the Cretan vernacular style on the far side of a small river. The inn was within shot of the bare limestone hillside in which the cave was sited.

Two hours later we sat over our evening meal, set among ancient stirrup-jars at The Aphrodite's tables.

Chapter IV

The Party Arrives At Eileithyia's Cave, Where Watson Gives Holmes a Talking-To

We set off early for Eileithyia's Cave. The day warmed up. Flies inflicted a bite like hornets on man and beast alike. The sun was almost directly overhead when the dragoman pointed to a dark patch on a hillside. "Our destination," he said. The crimson lining of a cloak flashed as the cave's occupant emerged. To my extreme relief I recognised my old comrade-in-arms. As I stared at him through my field glasses I wondered why he had struck so dramatic a pose. In private life, Holmes affected a certain quiet primness of dress – a tweed suit or frock-coat, the Norfolk coatee, occasionally an ulster. Now heads would have turned at the square blue spectacles and a cloak with a scarlet lining even in London's busy West End with its litter of theatres. On reflection, I realised Holmes had always opted for boldness in disguise. Not for him the self-effacement of the nightjar with its plumage drawn from the autumnal colours and shapes of its woodland habitat – bark, dead leaves, dappled shadows, the tips of dry bracken fronds. Even when he chose to disguise himself in the sombre black of a Non-Conformist Clergyman, with stock or cravat, the image he projected was extraordinarily compelling.

Holmes strode towards me with hand outstretched warmly. Hurriedly I started to alert him to my *nom de guerre*. He interrupted with the alarming words, "No need to continue with your subterfuge, Watson. I've informed every capital in Europe that you're here in Crete. Find a seat in the shade and sit yourself down. This landscape must remind you of your old Afghan days."

Almost before I could settle, he thrust forward a baked clay bar with script and what appeared to be numerals on it. "What do you make of that?" he asked.

I took the chisel-shaped object and examined it.

"I make nothing of it," I replied. "Perhaps you'll enlighten me?"

My comrade replied, “It’s an unknown script used to write an unknown language. Whoever deciphers it will become famous in the annals of code-breaking. Men could read these tablets once. It should be possible even after forty centuries for Mankind to read them again.”

“Holmes,” I said, unable to prevent a smile crossing my face, “if anyone can decipher it, it must be you. No one alive is fonder of enigmas and conundrums and hieroglyphics.”

“You may say that, Watson, but the cipher I solved in ‘The Dancing Men’ was infant’s play by comparison with this.”

I asked, “How will you start?”

“Somewhere on all these tablets must be a reference to the agriculture of the day – oxen, olive oil, figs, pistachio nuts – with pictographs for craftsmen – an armourer at Pylos, a purple-dye worker at Knossos – but unless I can work out where words start and end, there’s no way I can tell whether the system is logographic like Chinese, alphabetic like Persian, or, heaven help us all, syllabic like Akkadian. Nor even what the language might be – or whether these strange symbols are writing at all.”

“Now, Holmes,” I interrupted, checking the dragoman was out of hearing range, “at least I’ve discovered you’re alive. What of the *raison d’être* for your presence in the back of beyond? What of this Otto Müller?”

“What indeed?” came the rueful reply. “He’s disappeared from the face of the Earth. No one has been reported charting the bays and inlets. It’s possible he gained the information Berlin wanted and has been whisked away. Müller’s not new to this game. The charts he made on his expedition to Waziristan are the epitome to geographers – and to military planners. The ruthless part he played in Peking in drawing up the Boxer Protocol alongside Alfons Mumm von Schwarzenstein three years ago has yet to come to the eyes of the world.”

Apologetically Holmes continued. "If Müller's still here, I may have put your life on the line too. I had to try to unnerve him in the hope of flushing him out. I needed to declare my presence. It was I who instructed Milos to meet you at the dock. I told him, "Dr. Watson is my Boswell". The man then said, "If so, all of Crete will know you must be Mr. Sherlock Holmes!" To which I replied, "At your service!"."

I patted the pocket containing my service revolver. "I shall be ready, Holmes," I assured him. "As to Müller, I'm informed on no less authority than Milos that no one gets off the island unnoticed."

"If our German friend *is* here, it won't be for long," came the reply. "Last night a new type of Imperial German Navy submarine was spotted surfacing between the south of the Cretan mainland and the island of Gavdos. A Type U-1, an indication of just how important Berlin rates their agent's mission."

Holmes stood up and tapped the tobacco from his briar on the cave wall. "We can continue this over dinner. Let's summon the dragoman and set off for a meal of jugged Cretan hare. I'll join you on your pony for the ride to lodgings at The Aphrodite. Even their beds ought to be softer than the floor of this cave."

Holmes and I met in the morning for a warm breakfast drink on The Aphrodite's small dust-strewn terrace. His words upon greeting me took me aback. "Well, Watson," he remarked, "it's time to start the journey home. I deliberately revealed our presence to force my quarry to break cover. He hasn't."

I looked at him quizzically. "Are you accepting your mission has failed?"

"Otto Müller arrived – that I know – and then he vanished."

Holmes gestured at the forbidding landscape around us. "If he's gone to ground, ready to emerge the moment we depart, certainly I have failed..." His voice trailed away. He was looking hard over my shoulder, "unless..." I turned to follow his gaze. A man on a sturdy Anadolu Pony was coming at an overly-fast canter up the steep incline. It was Stavraki Aristarchi. As he approached he called out, "There's been a murder. A young shepherd boy."

Chapter V

The Murder Delays Our Return to England

We dismounted from the ponies and walked the final rough stretch of ground to a stone hut reminiscent of the hovels left from the clearances in the Scottish Highlands, ruins considered so picturesque by Victorian artists and visitors. A line of ripening tobacco straddled the doorway. A badging-hook lay against the outside wall. We had come across a scene of extreme pathos. A man looking more desolate than anyone could adequately describe was seated at a wooden table. A home-made lyre lay on it. The moment he saw us, he seized an antique musket and waved us away, calling out in Greek in a thick accent. We stopped while our dragoman went cautiously forward, assuring him we were "good people". "These *xenoi* have heard about your loss," he told him. "In fact," he added, pointing back at me, "this is a man of God, a Christian. He wishes to say a prayer over your son."

The dragoman relayed Holmes's first question. "No one," the man cried out in reply. "There was no one. Even with my old eyes I would notice a stranger at..." he pointed towards the hills, "...that distance."

He picked up a black-hilted dagger on the rickety table next to the lyre. The sturdy steel blade had only one edge which grew gradually thinner on approaching the tip, ending at a very sharp point.

"My son Nikos never went anywhere without this dagger. He wore it in his belt to withstand evil spells, but it was this blade which cut his throat. Look at the blood on it. Perhaps a demon made him do it to himself. Nothing can withstand the magic powers of the invisible world."

"Why would demons cast a spell," I asked, "if all your son did was tend your sheep?"

"Because he dared to enter the old stone quarry."

Tears began to drip from eyes displaying advanced opacification. "Even then, Nikos may not have been harmed if he hadn't gone as far as that chamber."

"Chamber?" Holmes enquired.

The father spoke rapidly to our dragoman, hand gestures inviting him to translate sentence by sentence.

"The boy came across it deep inside one of the abandoned stone quarries," Stavraki relayed. "The quarry consists of about one and a half of your miles of interlocking tunnels with widened chambers and dead-end rooms. Two of the sheep went into the tunnel mouth for shade. Something spooked them and they ran down into the depths. Nikos lit his lantern. He had a ball of string which he let out just like Theseus so he could find his way back. Finally, he caught up with the sheep in a great rectangular *tholoi*, a vaulted chamber like a Royal tomb. Twice the size of this house and lined with masonry."

Filtered through our interpreter's imagination the words became lyrical.

"In the centre, among a ring of stone libation vessels," Stavraki translated, "the boy saw a beautiful bowl in the shape of a duck made of rock-crystal. In the bowl was a cornucopia of golden necklaces with jewels which sparkled like the night sky, probably amethysts and diamonds and pearls, and above all the boy described the jewel-seal of a magnificent gold ring. The bowl sat out of reach on a nine-legged ebony table inlaid with ivory and gold, under a fallen stone too heavy to move. The stone had unintelligible letters cut into it. On each side of the duck, this far apart…" Stavraki spread his hands a pace or two, "…there were small bronze hinges and pieces of limebark."

"The remains of the coffer which held the bowl," Holmes remarked. "Stavraki," he continued, "he says his son made out the jewel-seal. Therefore, the ring was facing towards him?"

The father drew a piece of paper from a pocket and handed it to Holmes. Stavraki said, "That's the drawing the son made before the oil in his lamp began to run low and he drove his sheep back to the outside world."

I looked over Holmes's shoulder. Cut into the face of the ring was a tapering pillar. At its side stood a shrine-like building enclosing a tree. Holmes tapped the drawing. "This tree he's drawn, it's very like *Yggdrasil*, the sacred ash tree, the tree of life connecting the nine worlds in Norse and Teuton cosmology. The ash tree symbolises the tree which joins the three worlds, the underworld, the middle earth, and the spiritual realm. I have no doubt," he continued gravely, "that the jewel-seal means his son found the famed Ring of Knossos. If so, Nikos was the first human to set eyes on the ring for two and a half thousand years."

Holmes studied the drawing for a few moments more.

"I am certain of it," Holmes resumed. "Watson, see. Here's a god descending on a sacred obelisk which becomes his bethel. To the Ancients, the ring would bestow the power of Prometheus or Zeus on whoever wears it. They would also have believed it had the power of healing. To the romantic it would be the Ring of the Nibelung, fashioned by Rhinemaidens from divine light. The wearer would be assigned the power of Wotan or Alberich."

The old man rose abruptly to his feet. Our dragoman pointed to a mound of newly cleared earth some forty yards distant. "Come!" he beckoned. "We are being taken to where Nikos lies."

Stavraki and I knelt and cleared away the weightier stones placed to prevent excavation by wild animals, then scooped away the friable soil. We stared down at the thin torso. It had been a boy of about twelve years of age. His father had buried him in the son's treasured best clothes. A couple of inches of bare sunburned knees lay between the broken-down high boots and the skirt-trousers. I bent down over the child's head and recoiled in horror. "Holmes!" I cried back, "the boy's throat was slashed. Whoever did it made several cuts, one after the other. There can be only one reason to act like that."

In my time in the Army in India and Afghanistan, I had been called to many a corpse lying in the dust with its throat severed by a Pashtun blade. If the knife cut just the trachea below the larynx, the victim stayed alive but could no longer scream. A deeper cut and the carotid artery would be severed, preventing oxygenated blood from reaching the brain. A final cut to sever the jugular vein would bring unconsciousness and death. Done slowly and with surgical precision, as had been the case with the shepherd boy, the person would be gargling blood and coughing for many minutes, the whole while taking giant gasping breaths through the severed windpipe.

A red haze filled my vision. Holmes said quietly, "Watson, I'm to blame for this. I caused this boy's torture and death. My ruse in revealing our presence worked. It spooked Müller badly. It forced him to throw caution to the wind."

To maintain the fiction which had gained us access to the corpse, I performed gestures recalling the Padre giving the last rites to so many fallen comrades in skirmishes on the

North West Frontier. Holmes beckoned to our dragoman to return to the graveside and replace the soil and heavy stones. Staying on one knee at the grave, as though the dead boy could hear and understand English, the dragoman said, "Milos is the cause of all this. You wouldn't be dead if Milos hadn't tried his tricks on your family."

"What sort of tricks?" I asked.

Stavraki got to his feet.

"When Nikos came home and told the story, his father straight away wanted to make some money from it. He went to see Milos, hoping for a reward for giving him the information. Even a hundred *drachmae* would have been enough. Milos must have realised the story had the ring of truth, but said he'd only pay the father fifty *drachmae* and only after Nikos showed him the gallery. Everyone knows Milos is untrustworthy and the father refused. Milos said he'd give him time to think it over. Soon after, I saw Milos over at the Palace of Knossos talking to *Effendis* there. He was telling everyone he had discovered the location of the Ring of Knossos and would sell the information for a large sum of money. He came back and told Nikos's father a lie. He said the Englishman told him the real ring had been found many years earlier and had long since been spirited out of Crete. The one the son saw in the cave, Milos said, was therefore a fake. He would, however, do the father a favour. He would re-open negotiations with an offer of a hundred *drachmae*, saying he himself might get a hundred and fifty for the information by fooling one or other of the foreigners in solar topees at Knossos. Milos expected the father to capitulate."

Stavraki's hand gestured at the hovel.

"You can see how impoverished this family is. Soon the hungry season arrives. But Milos didn't take into account the father's superstitious fears. What if it *was* the genuine Ring of Knossos? What if, disturbed from its long sleep, the ring had the power to do bad things as well as good? Out of sheer dread, he ordered his son to refuse to tell Milos anything further. Evidently it was too late," Stavraki speculated. "Rumour had got around that a shepherd boy had reported locating a treasure. That must have been how the word got out to the one who did this."

Holmes addressed the dragoman. "Tell him we shall leave him in peace with his sorrows after one last question. Has he or anyone gone into those tunnels since…" he gestured towards the grave, "…since his son was there?"

The old man shook his head violently. "No," Stavraki relayed. "Certainly no Cretan would venture there. Tradition has it that in the quarry's depths, in a long sleep, live the Triametes, the strange three-eyed giants, both cunning and cruel. The third eye, on the nape of the neck, looks backwards. If anyone awakens them, he suffers a terrible fate. As Nikos did."

We left the man to his grief, once again seated at his table. Holmes deliberately slowed my steps until we were out of anyone's earshot. With an anguished look he said, "Watson, incredible as it may seem, my brother Mycroft has made an ineffable blunder! And our War Office is the biggest fool in Europe! They believed Müller was here to prepare maps and organise fifth columns for when war breaks out between Germany and England. The true reason for his mission is completely different."

"What might that be, Holmes?" I asked, utterly confused.

"Erb's Palsy."

My jaw dropped. "Erb's Palsy?" I repeated, gaping at my companion. "What has an arm weakness to do with Müller's presence on Crete?"

"You're the medical expert," came the reply. "Tell me – exactly what is Erb's Palsy?"

"It's a paralysis of the arm caused by injury – specifically the severing of two of the upper trunk nerves."

"And the most common cause?"

"*Dystocia*. An abnormal or difficult childbirth. An infant's head and neck are pulled toward the side at the same time as the shoulders pass through the birth canal."

"And the prognosis?"

"Poor. The paralysis sometimes resolves on its own over a period of months, but mostly it leaves the patient with stunted growth in the one arm with everything from the shoulder through to the fingertips smaller than the unaffected arm. The sufferer is unable to lift the arm above shoulder height unaided, as well as leaving many with an elbow contracture."

"And who is the most famous – infamous – ruler in the world suffering from Erb's Palsy?"

"Kaiser Wilhelm?" I ventured.

"Exactly, Watson," came Holmes's response. "Müller's mission here has nothing to do with menacing England's sea-lanes to British India. It has everything to do with a Kaiser's desperate search for a cure to his palsied arm. An *opera-bouffe* dictator of a Central European Power believing a magnificent gold jewel-seal with representations of tree worship may have the magical ability to cure his palsy may seem far-fetched, but when Wilhelm was six months old, his doctors slaughtered a live hare and tied the flesh of the dead animal, still warm, to the infant's left arm as a poultice, hoping the vitality of the animal would transfer to Wilhelm. This they did twice a week for years. He's already been blessed with enough Holy Water to fill the Kaiser Wilhelm Kanal twice over. The Ruler of Germany believes some inanimate objects have magical powers, such as sacred trees, belemnites, meteor stones – or the gold Ring of Knossos. The Kaiser would know an archaeologist by the name of Heinrich Schliemann who wrote about excavations in Crete

– how he was searching for the ring. Schliemann believed it was buried around Mount Ida."

Holmes gestured back towards the broken-down cottage. "That's why Otto Müller was sent to Crete. The boy's murder proves he's still here. Even as we speak, he must be preparing to get his hands on the ring. The prospect of its return to the world has already brought death to an innocent child. Well-meaning men would try to use its powers for good, like the Ark of the Covenant, the Lance of Longinus, the Sword of Nuada, or even the Holy Grail, but clapped on the finger of a tyrant, it could become another Pandora's Box. The question is, where is Müller?"

Holmes stared out across the desolate countryside. My eyes followed his. No matter in which direction we looked, other than the old man's hovel, there was nothing indicative of human activity.

With his brow more furrowed than I could recall, Holmes swung himself up into the saddle. Then his head turned abruptly. He pointed towards the mountains. I climbed on to my own horse and followed the direction of Holmes's finger. Rising from a plateau above the weathered ridges was the top of a tall tower.

"Toplou," Stavraki replied. "The Great Monastery. That's the belfry. Very high. It was also used as an observation tower. A lot of killings have taken place there over the centuries. Now it's a backwater. I visited them last week. Sixteen monks and the drunkard Abbot live there."

"And the name Toplou?" I queried.

"The monastery 'with the gun' – so-called by the Turks for the cannon and cannonballs the Christians assembled to fend off Muslim attacks."

"Stavraki," Holmes ordered, "go back to the old man. Press him again. We'll wait here. When he went to discover why his son hadn't returned with the sheep, was he absolutely certain that he saw no one, no one at all?"

A few minutes later the dragoman returned, shrugging his shoulders. "No one," he said, "except what you might expect – just a *kalógeros*," he added.

"'*Kalógeros*'?" I queried.

Stavraki gestured up towards the plateau. "It's the name we use for those monks up there. It stands for '*beautiful ancient*'."

Both Holmes and I remained silent for much of dinner. Finally Holmes pushed back his dessert plate and said, "Nikos took a heavy risk in following those sheep. I doubt if any props are left holding up the tunnel roofs. Watson, what would happen if a rock-fall had trapped the child inside with no one knowing he was there?"

"Potable water would be the main thing," I replied. "Presumably the boy would have a small container, probably just a pint or two. Even if he lay completely still, it wouldn't last long. If he tried to clear the rock-fall, he could sweat that off in a quarter-of-an-hour."

"And then?"

"Dehydration would set in."

"Which would mean?"

"A water loss of only five to six percent will make him groggy. He would experience headaches or nausea, and possibly *paresthesia* – tingling in the limbs. By the second day the lining of the stomach would dry out and he'd experience dry heaves and vomiting. His tongue would swell, the eyes would recede back into their orbits. The mucus membrane might crack and cause the nose to bleed."

"By day three?"

"The final stages. The urine becomes highly concentrated, leading to burning of the bladder. The brain cells dry out, causing convulsions. At that point, without immediate rehydration, other major organs, including the lungs and heart, cease to function."

"Therefore?"

"Delirium, unconsciousness, and death. In awfulness, I rate death from dehydration at the very top."

After a short pause Holmes said, "I must be away for a day or two. Meantime, there's something important I want you to do. Get the dragoman to take you to the monastery. Become a guest of the monks at their communal dinner and surreptitiously count all the bearded heads. Keep up your guard. Take your service revolver with you."

I carried out Holmes's orders. I was back at The Aphrodite from the Toplou Monastery when a note arrived from him. It was written in the Dancing Men cipher familiar to me, a continuous stream of stick figures, each representing one letter of the alphabet. The message translated as -

Time to return to England. Pack up our belongings and pay hotel. If convenient come to the quarry at once. If inconvenient come at once anyway. Keep our ponies. Discharge the dragoman. We go straight on to the harbour at Candia.

I packed quickly and settled with Stavraki and paid the hotel's modest charges before going to the stables. The lunch basket was now down to one tin of Pressed Beef and two jars of Burgess's Genuine Anchovy Paste.

I was a hundred yards from Holmes when his words carried to me on the slight breeze – "Matches" – followed by a more insistent, "Do you have a box of matches?" He was standing at the opening of what appeared to be an artificial cave. Rough-hewn steps led down into the interior of the hill.

"I do," I called back, amused, assuming he wanted to light a pipe. He gestured behind him. "Dismount, Watson. There's something we need to do before we can leave."

A bony finger pointed at the tunnel floor. "Note the light green and brown colour of the dust. Magnesium iron silicate hydroxide. Ideal for camouflaging the fuse wire. Now it's just a case of lighting it. I would have done it by now, but I found that I was without matches."

"Fuse for what?" I asked blankly.

"To set off the charges. I bought a considerable length of fuse wire and a good portion of gun-cotton from the archaeologists at Knossos. To put them off the scent I told them I was on my way to dig at the ancient Minoan cave-sanctuary of Psychro. I've explored the tunnels and found the cavern, exactly as Nikos described it. There are only two possible approaches to it. The explosions the fuse will set off will bring down so much rock no one, including Otto Müller, would ever find their way back inside to the treasure. The Ring of Knossos can be left in its slumber to the very End of Time.

By the way," Holmes went on, "as a matter of interest, how many beards did you count at the monastery, in addition to the Abbott?"

"Seventeen ordinary monks, Holmes," I replied, continuing with, "Perhaps you could explain why…"

Before I could finish my sentence a look of alarm flashed across my comrade's face. "Seventeen *plus* the Abbott?" he queried. "Not sixteen? Are you certain?"

"Of course I'm certain," I replied.

"Quick, Watson – do you hear it? A horse is coming. We must get ourselves and the ponies into hiding. Those olive trees, mount and ride as though Lucifer himself were on our tail."

Chapter VI

The Seventeenth Monk Makes An Appearance

We crouched behind the gnarled olive trees at a distance above the tunnel entrance. My gluteal muscles pressed uncomfortably on the rock-strewn rise. A half-moon was coming up over the hill behind us.

"Holmes," I asked cautiously, "isn't this a waste of time? I mean, surely the very fact the boy's throat was slit means he refused to give away the location of the ring? Why else…?"

"We must assume the exact opposite, Watson," Holmes replied. "Nikos was given the *coup de grâce* precisely because his assailant had extracted the information he needed."

The sound of hooves on stony ground now filled the still air. Holmes and I rose in unison and slid fodder-filled nose-bags over our ponies' muzzles. An apparition came into view both absurd and sinister, a long-legged hooded monk on a donkey. He dismounted, hobbled the donkey at the quarry entrance, pushed back his cowl to reveal a mop of saffron-coloured hair, and consulted a scrap of paper. Crow-bar in hand and lamp above his head, he disappeared down the steps into the tunnel.

"The seventeenth monk," Holmes said, *sotto voce*. "Otto Müller."

I plunged my hand into a pocket and withdrew the service revolver. It had been within easy reach during countless moments in my years with Sherlock Holmes.

"I shall arrest him at once," I said.

"On what grounds, Watson?" my comrade asked.

Taken aback, I responded, "For the murder of the shepherd-boy, what else?"

"And you accuse him on what evidence?"

"Surely we can leave the investigation to the Crete authorities?" I exclaimed. "It's up to them to discover the evidence."

"From which witnesses? The father believes it was the work of three-eyed giants. You may take Müller at gun-point to the authorities, but once there he will claim diplomatic immunity. He would be on his way to Berlin in no time at all."

"What shall we do, Holmes?" I asked, deeply perturbed. "Surely we can't let him go free. You and I know he killed the boy."

"I have no doubt he did," came the reply, "or he wouldn't be here at the quarry, but it's perfectly clear it's out of our hands. We can do nothing, nothing at all. At most, we can alert the Cretan authorities to our suspicions. After that, nothing remains but to carry on to the harbour and board ship for England."

"For heaven's sake, man!" I exploded. "He slashed the throat of an impoverished peasant's only child. Nikos died after half-an-hour of the most heinous torture imaginable."

"Watson, however egregious his crime, Müller is not the point. The point is Due Process – Clause 39 of the Magna Carta! Wasn't it your namesake, a William Watson, who proclaimed *Fiat justitia et ruant coeli* – "*Let justice be done though the heavens fall*"? Id est, no rough justice! We cannot be the arbiter or ignore the law in the same way that Müller does. We must leave justice for the boy in the hands of the Cretan authorities. Come, my friend, it's time to go. By now, Müller will too far into the quarry to hear us. Even as we speak, he will be levering away with his crow-bar in the chamber itself."

"Quite, Holmes," I croaked. "Absolutely we should go! Your attachment to *Fiat justitiai* has convinced me. *Justitia's* the word!"

I plunged my hands into my pockets. "Oh my heavens," I cried out. "My father's pocket-watch! It must have dropped into the dust at the tunnel entrance. Wait for me, Holmes. I shall hardly be a minute, and we can pass by the authorities and press them to take Müller into custody. Or better still, leave my pony here and start off. I shall catch you up in no time."

Holmes was standing by the Anadolu Ponies holding their reins when I came hurrying back waving my heirloom. "Found it," I called out, urging him to mount. "I untethered Müller's donkey and sent it packing. Now we can return to London. On arrival, dinner at The Travellers on me? On Fridays they do an excellent *soupe au riz* with lemon, and *kebabs a l'huile*."

I mounted quickly, continuing my description of the Travellers fare. I was coming to the Horned Melon for dessert when a sound like the muffled roar of an immense bull belched from the inmost recesses of the mountain behind us.

"Great Scott!" Holmes exclaimed "So Theseus didn't kill the hideous Minotaur after all! Müller must have woken it up."

"A serious blunder on Müller's part," I nodded.

I fingered the box of wax vestas in my pocket, freshly depleted by the two matches it had taken to set the fuse alight.

το τέλος

NOTES

Toplou is a real monastery in Crete. The building was initially called *Panagia Akrotiriani* which means *Virgin Mary* of the cape. During the Turkish period the name was changed to *Toplou.* 'Top' means cannon because a cannon was stationed in the monastery as a line of defence against the Turks.

'The Creeping Man' (1923). Excerpts: '*A man named Trevor Bennett, the personal secretary of one Professor Presbury, comes to Holmes with a most unusual problem...'*
'Holmes also comes to realise, by connecting the professor's thick and horny knuckles, his odd behaviour, the dog's attacks, and the use of the creeper, that the professor is behaving like a monkey.'
One of the oddest of twelve short stories by Arthur Conan Doyle in 'The Casebook of Sherlock Holmes'

The Police Gazette. Sherlock Holmes's favourite weekly magazine. Formerly known as the 'Hue-And-Cry'. In Charles Dickens' *Oliver Twist*, the criminal Fagin is depicted 'absorbed in the interesting pages of the Hue-and-Cry'. It contained information on wanted criminals, crimes committed, criminals who had been apprehended, missing persons and even such events as the penal transportation of criminals to Australia.

Otto Müller. Between 1900 and 1914 Watson was no less prone than anyone else to contemporary paranoia about the German Kaiser's spies in every port and community in United Kingdom which became dubbed 'Spy fever'. Even men's barbers of German nationality in Britain's towns (especially ports) suffered through rampant Germanophobia, coming under great suspicion as a likely part of a fifth column. Letters pages of national newspapers like *The Times* were flooded with patriotic urgings to make 'timely preparations' to meet the enemy threat. William le Queux's '*The Invasion of 1910*' became – and remains - a famous example of 'invasion literature', describing a sizeable and heavily-armed German force landing on the East Coast of England.

facile princeps. 'Easily the first.' Said of an acknowledged leader in whichever field.

Thalassocracy, also thalattocracy. A State largely composed of maritime realms, a seaborne empire.

Caoba. Also known as Burger. A white wine grape of French origin.

Andolu Ponies. A Turkish breed developed over 1,000 years ago. Often seen in Crete and known for their speed, endurance and hardiness.

Xenoi. Singular *Xenos*. A word used in the Greek language from Homer onwards. The standard definition is '*stranger*'.

το τέλος 'The End.'

The Strange Death of an Art Dealer

Chapter I

The King of Scandinavia Makes an Unexpected Visit

I held my umbrella aloft. Continuous showers throughout the capital that day had caused pedestrians to leap aboard every conveyance, myself among them. Eventually I reached Baker Street and crossed the pavement to the safety of our door. As I entered the hallway, and without the slightest warning, my frame was suddenly shoved violently to one side, spinning me like a coracle in the wake of a twelve-thousand-tonne Cunarder. I looked up in time to see a figure flying past me and up the stairs, his blue cloak flapped open like the wings of a giant Urvogel. With an immense final bound, the intruder reached our quarters and barged in without a knock. I rushed up after him, my heart thumping.

In the sitting room, the man who had treated my presence downstairs with such hauteur stood towering over Holmes. One huge hand was wielding a large photograph like a sword of Damocles, the other clutched a pink envelope.

"Come, Watson," Holmes called out, with the easy air of geniality he could so readily assume, "I believe you know our guest?"

I had recognised him at once – the King of Scandinavia. Swinging his cloak from his shoulders, he said, "Apologies for brushing you aside, Dr. Watson, I was in a hurry. Once more I have travelled all this way for the sole purpose of consulting the keenest mind in Europe."

At our last encounter two years earlier our visitor had been the Crown Prince of Scandinavia. Then as now, the dark rings under our visitor's eyes were those of a man weighed down by some great anxiety. Since then, he had inherited the throne. He was now the King.

"Perfectly understandable, Your Majesty," I countered. "It's good to see you again."

"Gentlemen," Holmes remarked, "shall we all take our seats? Your Majesty, Watson and I will be interested indeed in discovering the reason you've obliged us with a second visit. Are we to take it your reputation is once more in jeopardy?" Looking upwards with a slight smile Holmes added, "and that it may have something to do with the items in your hands?"

"It is, and they do," came the terse reply, the monarch's expression one of deep distress. "Both occasioned by the cruellest of adventuresses, my former paramour, Enid Westburton."

He thrust the photograph into Holmes's hand. "Once more she is blackmailing me with another of these!"

The King pushed a pink envelope into Holmes's other hand. "And with this."

Holmes placed the picture on a small table in front of him and read the letter.

"Your Majesty,' Holmes continued, "I assume we are about to hear why, in view of this note, you haven't yet handed over a sufficiency of your great wealth to satisfy the demand it spells out, thereby being done with the matter?"

"Sir," came the King's piteous cry, "I believed the affair was finished two years ago. I trusted that was the end of it. But apparently she holds a number of other photographs, any one of which would serve as proof of my youthful indiscretions. The she-devil may have kept a hundred of my letters and ten – even twenty – such photographs taken during our time together. She can blight my reputation for years to come."

His face reddened. Tears welled up in his eyes. "To think she gave her solemn word she would never besmirch me again with such evidence of our affair, and yet here she is – "

His voice trailed away.

I expected to see Holmes's patience crumble under the rambling narrative. On the contrary, he listened with the greatest concentration of attention. Once read for a second time, the letter was folded and returned to its pink envelope.

"Rest assured, Your Majesty," Holmes said soothingly, "Watson and I are ready again to assist you in any way we can. Let us continue."

Holmes pointed to the photograph. "Now, Your Majesty, take a last look at this before you leave it in our safe hands."

"If I must!" the King cried. He gave the most cursory peek at the image before flinging it back.

Holmes passed the photograph over to me. Two people were portrayed in an elaborately decorated setting. The then-Crown Prince in the full dress uniform of his House, replete with insignia, sash, belt, and lapels, was seated on a bench of Ceylon ebony. He held the head of a sword in his left hand and a hat with plumes in his right.

The picture was exactly as I remembered him from our meeting several years earlier, before the cares of his position had aged him. It was the other figure which caused my sharp intake of breath. A woman lay full-length before him on a rich carpet looking up at the Prince in an adoring fashion. With the exception of jewellery and a pair of oriental slippers on her feet, the voluptuous body was completely nude.

"You see what I mean, Dr. Watson," the King bellowed. "The vixen has broken her word."

"You, sir, we recognise at once," Holmes broke in, "but be so kind as to confirm for us the woman stretched out along the floor is Enid Westburton, *née* Bainbridge."

"Who else!" came the mournful reply. "That profile! The hair adorned with a simple gardenia. The Gypsy ring in her ear. Who else could it be? You see her right arm? I gave her that bracelet at the very height of my unreasoned passion. The gift was made to my design by the Royal jeweller – fiery-red pryopes of the finest quality sourced from the mines of Meronitz, the emeralds from South America at a price even beyond the normal reach of princes.

For three years I showered her with such evidence of my infatuation – parcels of precious jewels, the finest silks and furs. Even – " He groaned in unexpected self-mockery. " – a dressing-table made of Purple Heart wood from the island of Trinidad, equipped with a secret compartment to hold the rings and bracelets and intimate items such as that…that…" He spluttered, pointing at the bracelet in the photograph. "I tell you, gentlemen, she could make the part of Verdi's Lady Macbeth her very own. There must be something devilish in her, something I completely failed to see at the time, something stifled and dark."

"The letter," Holmes interrupted. "Have you read it in its entirety?"

With a sullen look the King replied, "In its entirety, no. You can see she made herself clear quickly enough. I was so shaken I ordered a coach and pair to bring me across the seas at once. Thus you see me here."

Holmes moved across to a cabinet. After searching through various documents, he pulled out a letter. He looked over at the King. "This is one of the notes she sent to you several years ago, and which you provided at the time. Watson," he called out, "please record both of these letters are written on fine-quality pink notepaper, with the same watermark and in the same swashbuckling black ink."

My friend returned to the photograph. Eventually he looked up and asked, "Your Majesty, does anything about the recumbent figure stand out?"

"I remember her breasts being rather smaller," came the reply, "but perhaps with the passage of time one's memory …"

He paused and sighed. Then, "Oh my God!" he exclaimed despairingly, "it could be a catastrophe! I beseech you, Holmes, sort this whole thing out. I can neither think nor sleep nor attend to any matter of State. It's enough to unseat my reason."

Holmes stood up.

"Your Majesty, let us know where we can reach you. From this moment on, the weight of the matter rests upon my and Dr. Watson's shoulders."

The King reached into a pocket and withdrew a small gold box.

"Mr. Holmes, this time, I shall insist on conferring upon you the freedom of my capital city which comes with this gold box, ready to be inscribed to record the occasion. If that is insufficient, you may ask for an entire Province of my Kingdom."

Holmes replied in a business-like tone, "Before that, sir, comes the case itself, and before that, the little matter of our expenses."

Speedily the King took a heavy chamois leather bag from under his cloak and dropped it on the table. "Shall we say a deposit of one thousand pounds?"

He swung round to the hat-stand and retrieved his cloak.

"Gentlemen," he intoned, "You have *carte blanche*. I'm staying at the Langham Hotel. Do whatever is necessary." In a change of tone he added, "You *must* succeed. I was prone on the previous occasion to let the better side of my nature prevail. Now too much is at stake. I have a dynasty to protect. My throne may not withstand the exposure of my past. Republicanism runs deep in Scandinavia."

He paused for a moment, glancing in my direction. "You look dubious, Dr. Watson. The Lands of the Scandinavian Crown may not be the equal in wealth and extent of the India of your familiarity but for me they encompass the whole world. From here on in, the velvet glove must be ready to give way to the…" He paused, trying to think of the words in English. Failing, he spat out "*Eisenfaust*".

With a wry, "I believe I know the way out," he turned toward the stairway. Holmes called after him, "The letter asks for a large sum in *kruna* and several pouches of perfectly transparent diamonds with no hue or colour, each gem within a given range. Did you read that far? If so, have your brought the money and gems with you? I may need them at the ready if I'm to act as intermediary."

"I have them here, Mr. Holmes," growled the King of Scandinavia. "They are in the safe at The Langham, just in case you fail."

Holmes went to the top of the stairs. "If the author of the letter is within the grasp of England's Law, we already have enough evidence to go to the police."

"My dear Mr. Holmes," the King replied reproachfully, "*Of course* I know I could go to the police. However you must explain to me how would I profit if the author of that blackmail note was sentenced to a few months in prison while my own ruin must immediately follow from the publicity?"

From the window we watched the coachman pull open the crested door of the stately Canoe Landau. Our client clambered into the black Morocco leather interior. Pulled by a pair of horses, the wheels of the carriage rolled away down the street.

I had held my tongue during the discussion, having long ago learned to let Holmes take the lead on such matters. "You do know," I said eventually, "that Enid Westburton and her barrister husband …are dead? They died within a few months of their marriage. Their yacht sank in a terrible storm off the tip of South America and they must have drowned. It's that which makes this case so utterly inexplicable. A shiver went up my spine when the King waved the new extortion note at you. She couldn't possibly…"

Holmes nodded and stepped to his files, pulling a box of newspaper clippings off the shelf. "I remembered the reports immediately. Here's a cutting from *The Times* dated December 1884. '*Couple Lost at Sea*'. '*From our Buenos Aires Correspondent*'. It goes on, '*A tragedy is reported to have taken place. Mr. William Westburton, a barrister of the Inner Temple, and his wife Enid are reported missing off Cape Horn, believed lost in a storm while heading for Valparaíso aboard their yacht,* The Santa Margherita.'

Holmes continued, "A footnote by *The Times*'s legal correspondent stated that unless their bones are brought up in a fisherman's net, their fate remains in limbo until declared dead *in absentia*. According to friends conversant with English Law, it's generally assumed a person is dead after seven years given no evidence to the contrary."

He returned the cutting to the box, adding, "Nothing's been heard since of Mr. and Mrs. William Westburton. I suggest it's a case of *Defuncti sunt*."

"Then why – ? " I began.

Holmes interrupted, reaching for his coat. "Watson, our Royal client displays scant consideration for how little we have to work with – no footprints on the lawn, no codes or ciphers, no cigarette ash, no dogs, no corpses, no bloodstains. Just one jot – the letter – and one tittle – the photograph. A stroll would help clear the mind. I suggest we forego Mrs. Hudson's wonderful Scottish fare and lunch out today at the King of Scandinavia's expense."

"Excellent suggestion!" I replied. "Will it be off silver at Simpson's? I dream of their joint of beef."

"Nothing quite so exotic until the conclusion of the case," came Holmes's cheery reply. "More like steak-and-kidney pudding off tin at Ye Old Cheshire Cheese on Wine Office Court. Bring the photograph. After lunch, hurry it over to Gregson at the Yard. Ask him what he makes of it. I suspect he might have an idea…"

Chapter II

I Take the Blackmail Photograph to Scotland Yard

Holmes and I maintained a reflective silence during the walk to Wine Office Court. My mind went back two years to the rather straightforward events concerning the earlier attempt to blackmail the then-Prince. Perhaps we should have realised the affair wasn't truly finished.

We parted company after a veritable feast of diced beef and kidney, fried onion, and brown gravy. Later, at Scotland Yard, I swore the admirable Inspector Gregson to secrecy and handed him the photograph. On my return a few hours later, Holmes was at the dining table, the two pink letters in front of him held down by the gasogene bottle against gusts of air from the open window.

I opened my mouth to speak, but Holmes's hand rose swiftly. "Watson, this is a time for observation, not for talk. Take another look at this letter. This first is unquestionably written by Enid Westburton."

"What am I to look at?" I asked.

"At the way it's signed off," Holmes replied.

"'*Enid Westburton, née Bainbridge*'," I read out.

“Now,” Holmes went on, “what about the latest letter. How does it end?”

“With ‘*I have the honour to be Sir Yours obediently, Enid*’,” I replied.

“Exactly! Doesn’t that seem peculiar? ‘*Yours obediently*’? Remember, it’s for the King’s eyes only, someone she knew intimately, but it ends with a salutation as stiff as if the letter-writer were addressing Albert Edward, the future King of Great Britain. Why?”

I had no answer.

I spent the evening flicking through articles in *The Journal of the American Medical Association.* A heart specialist, Professor Robert H. Babcock, recommended prolonged physical repose in cases of valvular disease. My experience with such patients was quite the contrary. The striated cardiac muscle degenerates under prolonged rest. I resolved to contradict the Professor’s conclusions in a Letter to the Editor. I threw the journal down. The chimes from our housekeeper’s spring-driven regulator wall clock told me it was a quarter-to-midnight.

“Time for me to turn in,” I said.

Holmes was bent over his Powell and Lealand No. 1 microscope, tucked among an array of Bunsen-burners, glass tubes, and pipettes at the chemical bench. A thought occurred to me.

“Holmes,” I said. “You are keeping in mind that Enid Westburton and her husband are dead, aren’t you?”

“*Defuncti sunt*,” Holmes said. He looked pensively at the recent letter. “Thank you, Watson. Now may I wish you good-night.”

I lay awake well into the early hours. I could see the possibility – probability even – that the King himself, tucked away in Scandinavia, might have had no knowledge of the tragedy. No courtier or Scandinavian newspaper would mention the obscure names of William and Enid Westburton. But what was going on in Holmes's mind? He seemed deliberately to be ignoring the information about the sinking of the *Santa Margherita*. If so, why? What good reason could he have had to do so? Why had he repeated the words *defuncti sunt* - *They are dead* - in so dubious a tone? Was my Latin at fault – or my assumption of their deaths? Why had he made so much of the way the two Westburton letters had been signed? I vowed to have it out with him over breakfast.

I awoke with the dawn and washed and dressed immediately. Holmes was already eating breakfast. He greeted me with an air of geniality.

"I have a question for you," he began. "Shall we agree you are more of an expert on wedding procedures than I?"

"We can agree on that, Holmes, yes," I nodded.

Holmes continued, "Then tell me, what first steps are required which lead eventually to the Altar?"

I filled a plate with our housekeeper's devilled kidneys and kedgeree.

"My dear friend," I replied, "if you are for some reason referring to the marriage of the late Enid Bainbridge and the late William Westburton which occurred shortly after the lady's first attempt to blackmail the King, matters would have typically commenced through an exchange of formal letters between the groom and the vicar."

"Let us assume I am indeed referring to that marriage," Holmes responded. "Where do you suppose the correspondence related to it would be held? Tucked away in a tin box in a crypt?"

"No, Holmes. Almost certainly in a file in the vicar's study," I replied.

"Then I'm in need of your help, Watson. It's imperative to get into the vicarage of the church where the two of them were married and examine one of Westburton's formal letters. The solution to the case may depend upon it."

A cab discharged me at the vicarage of St. Catherine's Church. A double carriage-sweep lead through lawns and past an immense Cedar of Lebanon. A smiling plump house maid showed me to the study. The vicar stood up, stretching out a hand.

"You must be Austin Bidwell," he said, "I'm William Barker."

The vicar withdrew a letter from an overflowing file. "I have your letter here. You indicated a wish to get married in St. Catherine's and you are a resident of this parish."

"Correct, Vicar," I lied, "even as we speak, my fiancée is choosing the month and day of our wedding."

"Not in May, I hope!" the vicar joked. "Remember, "Marry in May and rue the day"."

"Then certainly not May…" I began.

Our conversation was cut short by a loud hub-bub between the house maid and someone at the front door. The vicar jumped to his feet.

"Do excuse me, Mr. Bidwell, it seems I must intervene on Miss Nightingale's side. Probably beggars again. They can get very aggressive. I shan't be a moment."

Virtually in step, I followed him as far as the study door and eased it shut behind him. The vicarage's front entrance was visible from the study window. Gesticulating dramatically, now almost nose-to-nose with the Reverend Barker, was a figure in clerical garb replete with broad black hat, baggy trousers, and white tie – a disguise Holmes particularly favoured. He was usually the very model of an amiable and simple-minded Nonconformist clergyman ostensibly from the village of Rollesby on the Trinity Broads, except that now there was a difference. The amiability was completely absent. His facial expression had changed utterly from one of benevolent curiosity to one expressing utmost scorn. I heard him shout, "My dear Vicar, yes you are! Don't deny it! I have myself just returned from Cape Colony. I have no doubt that you are tolerant of Zulu polygamy! Clearly you are a heretical follower of Bishop Colenso!"

"I am most certainly not, I repeat, *not*!" the vicar was protesting loudly.

"Yes, you are!" insisted the newcomer, "I would wager half of my stipend that you have the Bishop's confounded work *The Pentateuch and the Book of Joshua Critically Examined* on your shelves! Let me in to see if I'm right, sir!"

"I do not, sir!" the vicar shouted back. "And I shan't let you in! You are a lunatic! You may leave my door immediately, never to darken it again, d'you hear?"

"I shall not move one foot from here, sir," came the angry response, "until you confess!"

I hastened to the vicar's desk. The sounds of two people pushing furiously at each other continued, their voices combining with Miss Nightingale's, the tone of all three rising ever-higher. At *W* under '*Marriages*' I found correspondence from William Westburton dated two years before. It had been signed off with "*I have the honour to be Sir Yours obediently...*"

I made for the door. The Nonconformist clergyman had beaten a retreat. I promised the badly-upset vicar I would be back in touch with dates for the wedding (other than May) and hurried to catch up with Holmes now lurking in the garden behind the Cedar of Lebanon.

Chapter III

We Meet Inspector Gregson at Simpson's in the Strand

On the morrow I was awaked by a familiar rat-tat-tat on my bedroom door. It was flung open to reveal Holmes waving a telegram. "Our Scotland Yard inspector has some information for us. I've arranged a quiet table at your favourite temple of food, Simpson's."

A few hours later Holmes and I met the tow-headed Gregson in the restaurant foyer, his hat in one hand, a package the exact size of the photograph in the other. He was in mufti, his pea-jacket and cravat giving him a decidedly nautical appearance. He looked pleased with himself.

"Well, Gregson," I asked, "what have you got for us? Can you confirm the woman lying on the carpet is Enid Westburton?"

"I've no idea if Mrs. Westburton ever allowed herself to be captured *au naturel* like that," came the unexpected reply.

Frowning, I pointed at the package containing the photograph. "Surely that's proof enough!"

"I'm afraid not," Gregson responded.

We were shown to a corner table.

"I can confirm the woman's head with the ear-ring is Enid Westburton's," Gregson resumed. "Equally I can confirm the arm with the bangle is hers as well. But I cannot confirm," he tapped the package "that the torso is Enid Westburton's."

Holmes broke in, "Watson, that could explain why our client reported her rather more buxom than he remembered."

The table fell silent at the approach of the *maître d'hôtel*.

Gregson chose the roast beef, Holmes the woodcock. I opted for the smoked salmon and my favourite dessert, the treacle sponge with a dressing of Madagascan vanilla custard. The *maître* retreated to the kitchen with our orders.

Gregson continued, "We did exactly what you asked, Mr. Holmes. The Yard has developed twenty forensic techniques, from the packaging to the shadows. Only if all twenty are completely consistent will we declare the photograph real, but in this case…" He glanced my way. "Mr. Holmes, may Dr. Watson have the momentary loan of the ten-power magnifying glass you always have with you? Thank you. Dr. Watson, do me the kindness of looking at the woman's hair."

I held the glass over the luxuriant dark hair spilling on to the shoulders.

"What am I to look for?" I asked at last.

"The reflection of the light on her hair and the ear-ring," came Gregson's reply. "Specifically the source of the light."

"I would suggest it was sunlight through a window this side of where she's lying," I replied.

"Good!" Gregson exclaimed. "And now the bracelet. The light scattering off the brilliants. The source of the light – still the same window?"

"It can't be," I responded. "It's coming from the other side."

"Bravo, Doctor! Now if we take the light reflected from the skin of the legs and the naked buttocks and back, you'll see it's coming from yet a third direction – from above. Very likely a skylight. This print cannot be from a single photograph. What we have here, gentlemen, is an ingenious example of combination printing. The head and right arm are from one plate, but they've been added to a torso and legs from a separate plate – the latter a work we have identified as '*Reclining Female Nude Artists, Study, Dorsal*' by the artist-photographer Oscar Rejlander."

"So all Holmes and I have to do – " I began.

Gregson interrupted, his face creasing into a grin "– is to confront Rejlander and ask who bought the *Reclining Female Nude Artists* study plate. Confronting a suspect is always a good idea, Doctor, a splendid idea. Alas, Rejlander died not long after making that study. His body lies in an unmarked grave in Kensal Green Cemetery, near Isambard Kingdom Brunel."

"Then who made this brilliant fake, Inspector Gregson?" I asked.

"One living artist-photographer possesses the skill," he replied. "We believe that he may also be the owner of the plate. Rejlander died leaving little money, not even enough for a tombstone. His widow was obliged to put his earlier works up for auction. A job-lot of plates was bought by a certain society photographer – but there's a problem in assuming he's the perpetrator of a fake of this order. You'll see why in a minute, when I come to his name.

"As I am singing for my dinner, gentlemen," Gregson went on, "I've another fact of relevance to your case – the camera used by the draughtsman. The camera which created this photograph – or so my experts tell me – held a twenty-by-twenty-four-inch plate. That size is both rare and expensive. We think it could only have been an Eastman Interchangeable View camera brought over from America. Even without a Beck lens or Laverne shutter, it would come with a heavy price tag. At least one hundred dollars." Gregson looked longingly at the slices of beef on the dish being placed in front of him. "Only one or two photographer-artists in the whole of England could afford that equipment and have the right skills to produce the work in question – one of them being the photographer of impeccable standing to whom I referred."

"Watson and I shall be very much obliged to you, Gregson," Holmes remarked, with a hint of impatience, "if you will now give us the photographer's name. You may then pick up your knife and fork and carry on with your lunch."

The inspector leant forward. "Alexander Berlusconi," he whispered. "It was he who purchased the Rejlander collection, though why in heaven's name he would associate himself with criminal activity of the sort you describe is beyond my comprehension. The walls of his premises are covered with studies of England's rich and powerful – aristocrats, Prime Ministers, leading names from the military, sciences, and arts. Even our Great Queen herself."

We hurried through lunch. Dessert behind us, we left the restaurant. Gregson bowed solemnly and strode off into a dense fog settling over the city. Back at 221B, I picked a red-covered volume from a line of books of reference beside the mantelpiece. Over the years my collection of the biographies of men of affairs, living or dead, had become so comprehensive it would have been difficult to name a subject or person on which I couldn't at once furnish information. Squeezed between Bell and Blackborough was an advertisement clipped from a national newspaper.

Old Photographs Enlarged

Old or faded carte de visite *or cabinet photographs may be enlarged and changed into valuable portraits, suitable when framed, to hang or stand in the drawing room.*

Photographs entrusted to Messrs. Berlusconi for this purpose are finished in black-and-white or watercolours.

"A faithful yet improved reproduction of a cherished original." – *Vide the Press.*

Specimens on view at Messrs. Berlusconi, 25 Old Bond Street, and 42 Pall Mall, S.W.

Chapter IV

Holmes Confronts the Society Photographer

The cab dropped us at the Messrs. Berlusconi Old Bond Street entrance. The studios were spread over three floors, joined by a broad staircase. There were reception rooms and dressing rooms, and two main day-lit studios equipped with good-quality furniture and props. Berlusconi was waiting for us in a small room at the top. He appeared nervous.

"Gentlemen, please have a seat. I look forward to taking your photograph. I presume that you are here for that reason? Am I to get a 'first' – namely the famous Consulting Detective together with his faithful friend, Dr. John Watson?"

Holmes shook his head, his expression cold.

"I'm afraid not, Mr. Berlusconi. Dr. Watson and I are here on a rather more serious matter. It seems you have recently used your very considerable skills to create an entirely spurious scene. Even as we speak, it is being used by a blackmailer to extort a large sum of money and precious gems from an eminent Central European personality."

The famous photographer blanched.

"Mr. Holmes!" he protested. "I am outraged! You come here to my premises to accuse me of a serious crime, one which would disgrace me both personally and professionally? Why, you only have to look to my reputation …" He gestured towards a large framed photograph deliberately placed on the wall behind his chair. It was of Queen Victoria in a black bombazine and silk dress. A satin bag at her side was embroidered with a poodle in gold. Beneath, the Queen-Empress had penned, "*To Mr. Berlusconi, for this study of me and its honesty, total want of flattery, and appreciation of character*".

"We appreciate your standing with the House of Hanover," Holmes responded, staring at the hapless man in a markedly unpleasant fashion, "which is why Dr. Watson and I are here rather than already at Scotland Yard. We offer you a chance to stay in Her Majesty's good books by confessing all and providing us with an explanation of your conduct. Then nothing will go outside this room."

Holmes turned to me. "Watson, how much time do we have before we solicit an appointment with Inspector Gregson?"

I pulled out my pocket-watch and gave it an exaggerated inspection. "It's now half-past ten," I replied, going along with the charade. "If we leave now we should be at the Yard in half-an-hour."

"Stop!" the agitated figure shouted. "All right – I confess. I was put under terrible duress. I had no idea of the man's intentions. I made a photomontage of a Teutonic-looking fellow covered in medals and epaulettes seated on a bench, with a nude woman lying on a carpet in front of him. I thought it was for pornographic purposes."

"And the name of the person who pressed you to do this?" Holmes asked, his voice deep with menace.

"The art dealer, Charles Augustus Howell," came the whispered reply. "I repeat, Mr. Holmes, I have no knowledge of the uniformed man in the photograph which he supplied, nor to whom the woman's head and arm belong."

He gave a shudder. Beads of fear appeared on the trembling upper lip.

He continued, "Howell glared at me with his cold, baleful eyes. It gave me a feeling of uncontrollable anxiety – the same sensation as if I were standing before the giant bird-eating spiders in the Regent's Park Zoo. On his instruction, I went through my rarest plates for a suitable nude."

He gestured towards a cabinet. “I came across a study made many years ago by Rejlander. All I did was leave the fellow on the bench and place the nude torso with a new head and right arm on the floor before him. After I completed the task, I told Howell to leave and never darken my door again.”

“Before we go, Mr. Berlusconi,” Holmes ordered, “tell us precisely why this man was able to persuade you to become involved in a criminal enterprise.”

“Howell had been sold some information about my father,” came the reply, “something so scandalous that if it came to light it would place a permanent slur on my family’s reputation and endanger my standing in London society.”

He pointed in the direction of Buckingham Palace. “Especially with Her Imperial Majesty. If you wish to move in Royal Society, you must make a great show of gentility. If you harbour any hint of a shocking or sordid secret about your personal life or that of a member of your family, you quiver in fear at the thought it may one day become public.”

“And the Rejlander plate?” I asked. “Where is it now?”

“I destroyed it in the hope of avoiding detection,” came the reply.

“Enough,” Holmes commanded, getting to his feet. “Come, Watson. A telegram to this Howell requesting an appointment is in order, I think.”

A knock came at the front door of 221 Baker Street, followed by the sounds of our housekeeper climbing the stairs. She came into the room with a card on a silver tray. It read ‘*You may call at 6.30 tomorrow evening – No. 6, Tilney Street, W1. C.M.*’

“Charles Howell lives at No. 6, Tilney Street?” I exclaimed. “He must be doing extraordinarily well. Wasn’t that once the home of the famous Georgian courtesan, Maria Fitzherbert?”

"The very same," came my friend's reply. He searched through his papers before finding a brochure. "In the event that we need to burgle the premises, let me read you a description of the house the last time it came up for sale. '*The grand suite embraces five drawing rooms, lofty and of the best proportions, all* en-suite*, and terminating with a conservatory, which entirely overlooks the Park. On the ground floor as the* salon à manger*, library, and breakfast parlour – nothing is wanting to render it an abode especially adapted to a family of consequence. There is an abundance of stabling, two double coach-houses, with servants' rooms*'."

Holmes stood up. His face wore the inexorable look he usually reserved for hunting down murderers. "I tell you, Watson, I've already developed a total revulsion for this fellow. Just to be completely safe, put a revolver in your jacket pocket. The Adams Mk III will do nicely. We may not require it, but on both sides the stakes are high."

Chapter V

Our Encounter with a Blackmailer

Shortly after six o'clock the following afternoon we set off for Tilney Street. The weather remained foul. After our meeting, I planned to go on to a performance of *The Sleeping Beauty.* On our way out of the house I knocked on Mrs. Hudson's door to borrow her opera glasses. The doors at No. 6, Tilney Street were pulled open as we leapt from the cab. We hurried in past the valet, keen to escape the squalls of driving rain. The butler came forward to take our coats and hats.

"Gentlemen, you are earlier than the Master suggested," he pointed out. "He may be engaged for a while. Please follow me."

We were led up a fine staircase via a succession of ornate rooms to the conservatory. I crossed to windows looking toward Hyde Park. In a direct line of sight across Park Lane was the eighteen-foot statue of Achilles, commissioned by the Ladies of England - a patriotic, upper-class society - in honour of the Duke of Wellington's victories against Napoleon. The sculpture was made from melted-down enemy cannon, the head modelled on the Duke himself, the body on a Roman figure on Italy's Monte Cavallo. I raised Mrs. Hudson's opera glasses. Some twenty yards from the statue a bedraggled figure with a camera on a bi-pod battled the heavy downpour and gusts of wind, his cape flapping wildly around his head.

"What do you see out there?" I heard Holmes ask.

"There's a hapless fellow trying to take photographs of the Achilles statue in the drenching rain," I replied. I passed over the opera glasses. "Here, take a look."

As he did so, our host entered. Despite a commanding role in the world of Fine Art, Charles Augustus Howell was only in his mid-forties, with a large, intellectual head, a round, plump, hairless face, and alert grey eyes behind gold-rimmed glasses. He advanced towards us, expressing regret at keeping us waiting. Holmes disregarded the outstretched hand, looking at him with a face of granite. Howell's smile broadened. He shrugged his shoulders. With a practiced dance-like step, he turned to take a seat. As he did so, the butt of a large revolver momentarily projected from an inside pocket.

"What brings you to my humble abode, gentlemen?" he asked. "Have you come to buy a Rembrandt - one of his self-portraits? Or are you hoping to view the Gainsborough, the '*Duchess of Devonshire*'?" at which he broke into a chortle. "If the latter, I'm afraid I can't be of help. I'm told the Duchess may as easily be in Chicago as here in Mayfair."

He spoke in a jesting tone, but there was no jest in his eyes as he looked at Holmes.

"No, we're not here in pursuit of a Rembrandt or the stolen Gainsborough," Holmes rejoined sternly.

"Then why are you here?" Howell retorted, almost insolently.

Holmes withdrew the pink envelope from an inside pocket and read aloud from the letter. "'*My dearest Sigismond, I believe you will recognise this photograph and the happy memories it evokes in me of our time together. I keep the picture in my dressing room. I never choose my evening's attire without stopping to look at it – and yet, curiously, when you were present with me, I scarce ever cast my eyes upon it...*'."

Holmes lowered the letter.

"Should I go on?" he asked with a cold look, "even though the words must be perfectly familiar to you?"

"Please, do go on, Mr. Holmes!" came the energetic response. "Yes, certainly go on! I'm finding this of extraordinary interest. I shall be especially keen to know who wrote it and for what purpose!"

Holmes continued, "'*Time has been good to you but unkind to me. My husband struggles to provide me with the small things which make life attractive. In return for the photograph, I ask only for a small part of what you have in abundance – wealth – but which I am sorely lacking (and am enduring penury as a result). Your assent or otherwise to my terms should be addressed to me at the Leadenhall Street Post Office, to be left until called for*'."

Holmes put the letter down. "Does it strike a chord now, Howell?"

"Sir," came the hurt reply, "it does not!"

Howell snatched off the gold-rimmed glasses. "Mr. Holmes, you astound me! I counsel you to inform the police at once! Surely you're not accusing me of some involvement – " He waved a hand at the table. " – with *that*?"

Holmes ignored the outburst. He retrieved the letter and recommenced, "'*I suggest 100,000 kronas and four or five of those delightful chamois pouches of colourless diamonds of yours. Each must be in the 80- to 120-carat range. Each must be uncut and unpolished, and not altered in any way after they were mined. A few uncut emeralds would be nice too. On receipt of the above, I shall destroy the photographic plate and have no further communication. You may rest in peace without hindrance'*."

Holmes looked up. His eyes fixed on the art-dealer. "Howell, we know you were the appointed go-between."

"I assure you," our host sang out, "you have the wrong person. I deal in *Art* – Caravaggios, Mantegnas, occasionally even a Poussin. I know absolutely nothing about this. Besides, you haven't revealed who wrote that letter. Perhaps the name is familiar to me?"

"The letter is signed '*I have the honour to be, Sir, Yours obediently, Enid*' – " Holmes replied, "– namely Enid Westburton, formerly Bainbridge, wife of William Westburton."

An exaggerated look of incredulity crossed our host's pudgy face.

"My dear fellow!" he exclaimed, "do you have a temperature? Are you at death's door with brain-fever? William and Enid Westburton were reported dead years ago, lost off Homos Island! I remember reading about it in the – "

Holmes interrupted savagely. "Enough, Howell! The game's up, as Watson can tell you." Holmes turned to me. "Can't you, Watson!"

Before I could compose an answer, Holmes continued addressing me. "That fellow in the Park, the one you observed just now – lurking at the statue pretending to be taking photographs of Achilles in the rain. Would you say he was in his late-thirties, approximately of my height, about six feet tall?"

"Holmes, to tell you the…" I began. Then observing the warning glint in the deep-set eyes I stammered, "Why, certainly…" I patted our housekeeper's opera glasses hanging from my neck. "Yes, I'd say late-thirties, about six-feet tall."

"Good-looking?" Holmes prompted.

"Yes," I replied. "In a dark, aquiline way."

"And moustached? I'm sure that you observed the moustache?"

"Definitely moustached," I agreed.

Holmes turned back to our host. "You see, Howell, the man taking a soaking in a thunderstorm hardly a hundred yards from here – the man no doubt waiting to rush in the moment he sees us depart – that man is none other than the erstwhile Honourable Member of the Inner Temple, William Westburton, husband of Enid Westburton. He is the man who, only a week or so ago, provided you with the bogus document that I have in my hand. You may or may not know that he forged it. The ostensible author, Enid Westburton, has nothing to do with this criminal affair."

"My dear fellow!" Howell exclaimed, the tone markedly less bombastic, "they do say ghosts wander around Hyde Park, but not usually in the rain! Must I repeat, the pair were lost off Cape Horn years ago. You must have seen it in *The Times*. They haven't been heard of since."

Holmes got to his feet. "We must go," he said to me. To Howell he said, "Enough of your banter. The King of Scandinavia has made my task eminently clear – find who organised the delivery of this letter so that man will then regret his criminal involvement for every minute of every hour of every day for the rest of his miserable life. The King's much-feared 'Iron Fist' will be released from its velvet glove. Your career as a blackmailer is about to come to an abrupt and well-deserved end. It may well mean five years in one of Her Majesty's gaols. If you continue to deny the fact of your involvement, Watson and I will now resume our journey to our friends at Scotland Yard and hand the matter over to them."

The threat had no effect.

"Then gentlemen," demurred our host, "the butler must bring you your coats and hats. I must not keep you a minute longer!"

The insolent tone grew in confidence. "Do please give my compliments to Inspectors Lestrade, Gregson, *et alia*, won't you?" he begged. "Tell them I'm sorry I can't be of more help in this very distressing matter, but there we are!"

At this he rose as though to see us to the door. Holmes waved a hand towards the luxurious reception rooms. "Watson, just think, the Howell we see before us, the Howell of open manner and exhaustless amusing talk, friend of Ruskin and Rosetti, is also Howell the master extortioner. Sculpture and Painting are his camouflage. It's as good a tale of villainy as has ever been recorded. Before we go to Scotland Yard we have another civic duty to perform. Scandal rags abound, brim-full with the latest assaults, outrages, tragedies, murders, and blackmailings, all delightfully described in lurid detail with illustrations to match. What a backdrop No. 6, Tilney Street will provide for the illustrations! We can readily break our journey to the Victoria Embankment. We must first drop by *Tit-Bits* and a few other sensational rags, ending up at *The Illustrated Police News*."

The words "scandal rags" transformed the expression on our host's face. Smugness changed to alarm.

"Now don't be so hasty, Mr. Holmes!" he gasped, rubbing a handkerchief across his gold-rimmed glasses. "All right. I shall own up – after all, I was merely the messenger in the prank – but in return you must promise me confidentiality. I know from first-hand experience a thing or two about the damage adverse publicity does to reputations. Yes, I knew Westburton during his days at the Inner Temple. I had believed him dead, so you will understand that when I came into this conservatory about three weeks ago to find him sitting exactly where you are, I nearly had a heart attack.

"Westburton was desperate. He forcibly pointed out how indebted I was to him. When he was at the London Bar, he managed to suppress very damaging evidence against me. Even now, if that evidence were to leak out, I could be brought before the Old Bailey on a charge that – well, I prefer not to go into it. More to the point, he promised me a choice of uncut gems if the enterprise succeeded. He told me that Enid was alive but desperate for money. He explained she had grown to regret her earlier leniency over certain photographs retained from her liaison with the then Crown Prince of Scandinavia. She regretted not asking for more – a large sum in money, for instance, and especially a pouch or two of fine raw diamonds and an assortment of Musgravite, Alexandrite, Red Beryl, and Padparadscha sapphires which the Crown Prince had in abundance.

"Westburton gave me specific instructions on the type of photograph that he wished to be prepared – he believed that I had the knowledge and contacts to accomplish this – and he added that a pink envelope would be put through my front door that same night containing a letter that she had composed. It wasn't to be opened by anyone before it was placed together with the photograph into the hands of the King at his Palace. Westburton's own involvement was to be kept secret. I swear that's all I did. Now that I think about it, I wasn't even the messenger. I was the delivery-boy."

As we went down the wide stairs to the atrium, Howell's voice followed us. "You take me by surprise in one respect, Mr. Holmes. I had no idea the letter was a forgery and that Westburton himself was the author. How clever of him."

The large entrance doors of No. 6, Tilney Street shut behind us. Holmes declared, "We have stopped the plot in its tracks, Watson. Our case is almost done, but – " He gestured towards the statue of Achilles, " – to quote the Iron Duke after the Battle of Waterloo, it was the nearest-run thing you ever saw in your life. If our blackmailer friend had held his nerve back there, we would have suffered a defeat. Our august client would have been given the choice of paying up multiple times over the years, or suffering excruciating loss of standing across the whole of Europe, possibly even his throne."

I pointed to the towering statue of Achilles. "How you identified the person with the camera as Westburton when I and the whole world thought him dead is unfathomable! Not once did the fellow have his face towards us."

"That's what I meant about the nearest-run thing, Watson," Holmes chuckled. "I haven't the faintest idea who the man with the camera was, any more than you do."

After a moment of stunned silence I asked, "Then how did you know Westburton was still alive?"

"I realised it moments after the King handed me the letter," Holmes replied. "The instant I saw the way it ended. That's why I needed to prevent you speaking. For Enid Westburton to sign off to someone with whom she had had an intense and deeply affectionate romance with '*Yours obediently*' was utterly out of custom. Even our Royal client would have smelt a rat if he had read the letter through to the end. If she'd composed it herself, the concluding words would have been quite different. Therefore, if she did not write it, certain deductions follow. Either she did die in a terrible storm off Cape Horn and the letter was forged *post mortem*, or she is alive but played no part in the plot. So I asked myself, who was the author? Who was close enough to Enid Westburton to have knowledge of her writing style?

Who spent time in the formal world in which that letter was composed – for example, that of lawyers and the Inns of Court?"

"Of course!" I exclaimed. "Westburton himself!"

"Just so," Holmes continued. "The letter is dated the tenth instant. Clearly newspaper reports concerning his death were extremely premature. At this very moment, I'll wager that Howell is apprising him of our meeting, and how – of course without the slightest cooperation from Howell! – Sherlock Holmes and Dr. Watson are closing in upon him. I'll wager there'll soon be a desperate hammering at our door. Be a good chap, Watson, and wave down a hansom. Let's make our way with all due speed through this wet Mayfair traffic to Baker Street. I'm overcome with curiosity on one point in particular. The letter itself was utterly compelling, but why, if Westburton forged the letter in his wife's name and style, did he end it in such a formal way? That blunder and that alone gave the game away."

Chapter VI

Westburton Returns from the Dead and Tells His Story

Holmes's surmise proved correct. Within minutes of our return to Baker Street, steaming horses pulled a cab to a halt at the front door. A frantic clanging of the bell followed. Mrs. Hudson let in the visitor. Upon Holmes's shout of "Come up the stairs, Mr. Westburton!" he rushed in.

"Mr. Holmes! Dr. Watson!" he cried out. "I am here to beg you to hear me out and not – "

"Pray, sir, take my friend's chair by the fire," Holmes interrupted, casually lighting a cigarette and throwing himself down into his own arm-chair. "Start at the beginning. I hardly need to inform a member of the Bar, even a drowned one, that he will have to offer up the most convincing explanation if my colleague here isn't to summon Scotland Yard to come and arrest the corpse on the spot. You won't be the first extortioner dragged from this room to the Old Bailey."

Westburton took my seat and, for the next twenty minutes, he poured out a story replete with human emotion and fallibility.

"When I first met my wife-to-be, Enid Bainbridge, here in London," he began, "she was living rather quietly, far from the life she had pursued just a year or so earlier on the Continent. I too led a prosaic if moderately successful life – living with my mother in Onslow Square, with chambers at No. 2, Buck Court. Then something utterly unexpected took place. Some weeks after Enid came to consult me on a private matter, I began to sense that I had a chance of gaining her hand in marriage. At first it seemed a fantasy – an impossibility – yet as the days passed, her early sentiment appeared to turn into something stronger."

My impatience and curiosity at the slow pace of Westburton's narrative overcame me. Risking Holmes's disapproval I intervened. "Mr. Westburton, I am agog to hear the story of your marriage, but first I have a question which needs clearing up. The world thinks that you and your wife are long dead. Can you explain how notices generating that belief sprang up in *The Times* and *The Daily Telegraph*, only months after your marriage?"

Westburton's face broke into a sheepish smile. "I can, Doctor. At your instance, I shall go into that now. During our brief courtship, Enid confided she had had enough of fame. She said it was nothing but an illusion. If – and it was then the word 'married' itself first came to her lips – if we were to get married, we should seek a life of the utmost privacy. She told me she had long wanted to visit the very tip of South America – she had read of the Tehuelche Indians of southern Patagonia and the flourishing society in the capitals of the

Argentine and Uruguay and Chile and Peru. I said surely her fame was such that the very name Enid Bainbridge – even if changed to Westburton – would be known even in such a remote corner of the world. She convinced me otherwise – that she could disappear into a peaceful life of obscurity, which was her greatest desire.

"So desperately had I fallen for her beauty and intelligence that regardless of the likely effect this exile would have on my own career I agreed. I went further. I told her, if you want the greatest anonymity possible and for it to last forever, we must disappear so completely that no one will ever come out to search for us. In short, we must fake our own deaths by combining our disappearance with her dream of a new life in South America.

"Over the years I had done a great deal of sailing in the dangerous waters around Cherbourg and the Channel Island of Guernsey. It seemed to follow naturally that we should look for a sturdy yacht in St. Peter's Port and sail her down to the South Atlantic. We put our affairs in order before taking a ferry to the island where we purchased a caique already fitted out for a lengthy voyage. Enid renamed it after the church of Santa Margherita, said to be where Dante married Gemma Donati in the thirteenth century. We loaded the *Santa Margherita* with all our keepsakes.

"Months later, we made landfall at Cape Tres Puntas, where we discharged the crew taken on for the crossing. Within days, to the fanfare of a brass-band at the dock, the two of us set off again. It was to become the last leg of our life as William and Enid Westburton. Soon we engineered the belief the *Santa Margherita* had gone down attempting a reckless journey around the Horn in weather of the worst kind. Under changed names for the yacht and ourselves, we sailed into El Callao, a stone's throw from Lima, but to the world we had been lost at sea."

The recollection overcame him. Tears welled up in his eyes. He sprang from his chair and paced up and down the room in uncontrollable agitation.

"From then on things did not go well," he continued. "You can have no idea of the transformation that came over my wife shortly after our arrival in Peru. It was as though she had changed not just her name but her personality. It gradually became evident she couldn't have been leading the modest life here in London I'd assumed. I expected us to settle into a quiet life – the quiet life she'd insisted she wanted! – whereupon I would build a practice. Instead, within weeks she became restless. Money was at a premium, yet Enid began spending frivolously, eating into what limited resources we had. She repeatedly asked why I wasn't bringing in the money she was used to. During one flare-up, she rushed to her things and withdrew an exquisite gold-enamelled-and-diamond ink stand in the form of a state barge which the King had presented to her so she could write her love letters to him. This was followed by a pair of ornate fly swatters studded with jewels which Ram Singh II, Maharaja of Jaipur, had bestowed on the Crown Prince, and he in turn on her.

"She accused me of gaining her hand in marriage under false pretences. She shouted, hadn't I taken into account her standard of living, her expectations of at least 'adequate' money when I forced myself upon her happy spinsterhood and lured her into marriage? Out came a heavily-jewelled ring which she flung at me with 'Why don't you go and sell this if you can't find the money elsewhere!'."

He paused, shaking his head at the memory. "Well, what a ring! Shakiso emeralds. Slightly bluish-green with vivid saturation. 'Glowing' would be the word. The ring had been given to the Crown Prince by the Ethiopian Monarch Sahle Miriam Menilek II. As I inspected it, my wife was shouting 'That's the sort of gift I'm accustomed to being given!'"

Westburton lowered his head, his face agonised. After a short pause he resumed. "The recriminations became a torrent. "I remember when the Archduke gave me this, and when the Crown Prince awarded me that, and when His Royal Highness presented me with this!" *etcetera*. Finally a kind of madness came upon me. I felt driven to prove that, come what may, I too was capable of giving her a bejewelled Indian this and an ivory Japanese that. But how was I to accomplish this? Even in a fit of insane rivalry with her past lover, the Royal personage, how could I promise her anything of the sort?

"To have once imagined my stuttering law practice could bring in the money necessary is beyond my present comprehension. I was still in the throes of adapting to an entirely different legal system – Peruvian law is based on the Napoleonic Code. Simultaneously, I had to learn not only Spanish but the Quechua and Aymara languages. Out of the blue, deliverance seemed to come like manna from Heaven. It started when one day I left my house for the Lima law courts. An anonymous note – in English – was pushed into my hand."

Westburton reached into an inside pocket and withdrew a scrap of paper. "Here it is, Mr. Holmes."

Holmes took it and for my benefit read aloud, "'*Your Excellency, if you are desirous of owning the largest emerald jewel in Peru, perhaps in the whole world, in three days' time go alone to the ruins of an ancient temple one hour's walk north-east of the village of Pachacamac in the Valley of the Lurín River. You will be met at mid-day, where the gem will be shown to you. It weighs more than two kilos. It is the lost sacred emerald of the Incas, the flawless Umiña'*."

"The largest emerald jewel in Peru – perhaps in the entire world!" Westburton repeated, his eyes burning with recollected excitement. "It was Kismet! My darling Enid and I were destined to stay together. If only I could obtain this emerald for a satisfactory price and bring it back to London, I could sell it anonymously – perhaps to an emissary of the Russian Czar."

Early in the morning three days later, Westburton had set off for Pachacamac. He was met there by an old man dressed as the priest of a temple. "We sat at the foot of a gigantic kapok tree hundreds of years old. The 'priest' told me that Umiña dropped from the sky in the body of a meteorite. For many years, the jewel was worshipped and kept in its own temple under the protection of the priests. Umiña reinforced the Incas' belief their gems were not just ornaments but precious gifts from the gods. Then the Conquistadors arrived, with nothing but contempt for religions other than Catholicism. When the priests saw how the Spaniards lusted after emerald crystals, they spirited Umiña away, just in time. The Spanish soldiers came and razed the Temple to the ground. For centuries the whereabouts of the sacred emerald remained a mystery, until this elderly priest himself stumbled across it.

"Show it to me!" I begged him. He brought out a jewel the size of an ostrich egg, carved in the shape of a human torso. He said his greatest wish was to rebuild the temple before he died. He would rather sell the Umiña emerald to a rich foreigner and use the money for that purpose than tell the Peruvian Government how he had discovered it in a special cavity built into the foundations of the ruined temple. He was certain government officials would sequester it and offer a pittance in compensation."

Westburton paused and looked at us. "Mr. Holmes, Dr. Watson, what I would give if every client I placed in the witness box was so skilled in deceit! The story was utterly plausible. The cost of rebuilding the temple would be the price I had to pay, but it would be nowhere near approximate to the fortune I could obtain for the jewel. He even suggested I should first take it to Jaipur, the historic pink city of palaces and forts where craftsmen could cut Umiña into matching emeralds and separate them into dozens and dozens of anonymous parcels. That such a suggestion came from a priest should have rung alarm bells, but I was too enraptured with gaining possession of such a jewel. I knew nothing about emeralds. Since then I have learned that many gemstones in the possession of the best-endowed museums or the richest collectors like Czar Nicholas or the Rockefellers are in reality fake.

Suffice to say, I went to every point of the compass to raise the money. I even sold the yacht which had brought us all the way to our new life in South America. I told my wife the boat had been stolen. At the 'priest's' insistence I assembled the payment in untraceable five-*peseta* silver coins. I pretended to Enid word had come of my mother's death, so I would need to return to England *incognito* to visit her grave. And that's how I managed to get away, bringing Umiña with me."

Holmes and I watched in silence while Westburton took some time to gather his thoughts.

"Then came the most bitter disappointment of my life," he resumed. "I arrived at the London docks. I hurried straight away to Bonham's auction house. In front of their gem specialist I unwrapped the emerald from its hiding place in the hollowed-out husk of the Copuazú fruit. He was barely able to suppress a smirk. Had I purchased it in Lima? he asked. He informed me I was at the very least the tenth foreign visitor to Lima to fall for this trick. Far from being an emerald crashing to Earth from the skies or transported through jungles from the renowned mines of Ecuador or Columbia centuries before, Umiña was chrysolite, probably quarried in Brazil, not even of gem quality. The specialist proved it to me with the 'fog test'. Breathing on an emerald for one second will produce a mist on the stone which – if the stone is genuine – will evaporate in almost exactly two seconds. By contrast, the mist on a fake emerald will take at least five seconds to begin to dissipate.

"Gentlemen, I don't need to tell you how long the fog lasted on 'the sacred emerald of the Incas', nor that I, like every one of those deceived before me, did not want the fraud brought to public attention. I was in a state of shock. I asked Bonham's to call me a cab. An hour earlier I had arrived at the auction house in a neat little landau. For my departure they ordered a spavined one-horse hansom driven by a brown-whiskered, no-coated cabman in a battered billycock. This modest transport befitted my dashed hopes of great wealth.

"Hardly able to contain his mirth, Bonham's doorman passed Umiña up to me, shoved back into the fuzzy skin of the Copuazú. I yelled at the cabbie to get me away as fast as he could oblige his horse, in whichever direction took its or his fancy. The nag made a great show of movement, but little progress. After a passage of who knows how long, a flash came to me, an ironic solution to all my woes. It rested squarely with the King of Scandinavia. A particular feature of my legal career and regular appearances at the Old Bailey was the way I accumulated all the resources for conducting a great criminal enterprise. Among my clients were courtiers, politicians, adventurers, and Fellows from my old Trinity College. Among the legal fraternity were members of the Bar and masters of the High Court. Best of all, there was a blackmailer over whom I had a hold."

Westburton turned his head to stare at the pink envelope. "Also for my purposes there was a former *confrère*, a barrister's clerk, whose skill in writing documents in my or any other hand was matchless. Many a time in my absence and for my convenience he composed and signed off legal letters in a hand so identical I couldn't later be sure which was his and which mine. I had a hold on him too. I knew that he had built a lucrative side-career forging historical documents to sell to the British Museum Library, using writing materials and self-duplicated inks from the appropriate period. He had a most profitable line in letters purportedly written by Oliver Cromwell in the summer of 1647."

Westburton pointed towards the envelope. "Over the next day or so I put the wording together, demanding 100,000 silver kronas and five pouches of uncut gems of the finest quality. I knew which stationer supplied Enid's hallmark distinctive black ink and pink stationery. I even went to Regent's Street to purchase a small bottle of her favourite scent for the clerk to spray on the paper. After that, it was simply a matter of a brief exchange of carefully-worded telegrams to set a meeting with the final link, the professional art dealer and blackmailer Charles Augustus Howell. Thus have I been brought to this pitiable pass."

With the prospect in mind of writing up the story one day, I asked, "The King was ordered to respond in writing *poste restante* to Mrs. Westburton at the Leadenhall Post Office. How would you have retrieved it?"

Westburton patted his jacket pocket.

"The fear that Enid might disappear without trace before I return home drove me to bring her passport with me."

Up to this point, Westburton had been staring into the embers. Now he looked up. "Tell me, Mr. Holmes, what gave you the clue that the letter wasn't from Enid herself? Was the clerk's calligraphy less than perfect?"

"The script was flawless," Holmes replied. "Even when I compared it to the writing style from your wife at the time of your marriage I could find nothing suspicious."

"Then please enlighten me. How did you – ?"

"A blackmail letter is a most intimate form of communication, penned for the victim's eyes only," Holmes responded. "'*I have the honour to be, Sir, Yours obediently*' is hardly the signature of a courtesan to a former Royal lover."

I explained how I had seen a sample of one of his own letters in the vicarage at St. Catherine's, "which ended with exactly the same wording."

Holmes then passed the extortion letter across to our visitor. "I haven't set eyes on this letter until this very minute," Westburton murmured. He replaced the letter in its envelope. "I now see that the clerk simply wrote the style of ending he knew from fashioning so many of my more formal letters."

His voice was weary. "A blunder indeed. I should have checked the letter before it was sent, but rather than risk delay, I ordered the clerk to complete the missive and take it straight to Tilney Street. Time – or rather, the lack of it! – was of the essence. I was obsessed with hiding my presence in London. The longer I stayed, the greater the chance I'd be unmasked. Howell assured me he would engage a courier as soon as the photograph was complete, to expedite the letter to the King."

Holmes nodded. "What happened to the original photograph, the one which caused the Crown Prince so much panic?"

Westburton grimaced. "One afternoon I came back to our house in Lima to find that my wife had gone out. I was gripped by the greatest fear that she was preparing to leave me. Remembering where she'd hidden the Emperor of Ethiopia's emerald ring, I searched her things. Finally, before my disbelieving eyes, was the infamous photograph. I hardly had time to steal a glance at it when the sound of footsteps came from the stairs. Hurriedly I returned it to the hiding-place and flung myself on the bed as though asleep. When I had a chance to look for it again, it was gone. I never saw it again. When I needed to provide a photograph to Howell, the only one of Enid in my possession was a perfectly demure picture she had left at my quarters in the Inner Temple early on in our courtship. She was in evening dress, seated on a bench, wearing the ear-rings and a bracelet given to her by the Crown Prince."

Holmes murmured, "Which Howell took to Berlusconi to be altered."

Westburton nodded. "That was the photograph handed over to Berlusconi."

I broke in. "What made you take it for granted the King would still be willing to pay a fortune for it? He had long since married. Why do you suppose he isn't calm and reflective about his past – sanguine even – these days?"

Westburton smiled. "I ask you, Doctor, how calm and reflective would you be if the Chusseau-Flaviens Agency distributed such a photograph to every newspaper across Europe, the Orient, the United States, and elsewhere? You yourselves might have come across it in *The Illustrated London News*. Yes, I do believe the King would have paid almost anything, Doctor – if Mr. Holmes here hadn't intervened."

He continued, "The Crown Prince is now King and married. He and his Queen have produced a child. He would wish to protect them from a scandal which would rock society if such a photograph were to become common currency in the popular newspapers. Besides, the King is richer than ever, his new family the wealthiest and most glamorous Royals of them all. They own eleven castles and palaces, every one of them set in immense and fertile estates. Not even the Romanovs compare."

A long silence followed. Holmes puffed at a cigarette and gazed down into the fire. The silence was finally broken by the creaking of his chair as he leaned forward, pushing the pink envelope towards me.

"Alarums, Watson," he murmured, "but no lasting harm."

He pointed at the flames flickering in the grate.

"Westburton, no doubt Dr. Watson has your permission?"

"He does, Mr. Holmes!" Westburton exclaimed, his eyes shining with relief. "I shall be glad to see the last of it."

The envelope caught fire at the edges. Within seconds the coals had consumed the missive. Only the faintest sniff of Enid Westburton's favourite perfume lingered on in the sitting room air.

Chapter VII

The Hereditary King of Scandinavia is Given the News

The following morning I came down to breakfast to find Holmes in buoyant mood. I greeted him with a concern which had pressed in on me during the night. What did he intend to do about William Westburton? "After all," I said, "here's a man sworn to uphold the laws of England, a Member of the Bar, an Honourable Member of the Inner Court. Yet we have now burnt the most significant piece of evidence that Scotland Yard would need to – "

"It was a three-pipe problem," Holmes broke in, "but I have decided Westburton's fate. He has learnt his lesson. However, that leaves a larger concern. What's to be done about Howell? He's equally complicit, yet he remains untouched – a deadly virus at the heart of London Society. You saw it was a matter of complete indifference to him when we threatened him with Scotland Yard. He's perfectly aware that blackmail remains outside the ambit of the criminal law."

"Holmes, your knowledge of the Law is greater than mine. Isn't there any kind of charge which might succeed against him?"

"Larceny by Extortion, perhaps," Holmes replied, "but he would plead he was merely offering the King an item of great sentimental value in the hope of a suggested reward."

Holmes reached for his tobacco pouch and blackened briar. "By contrast, Westburton's fate lies entirely in our hands," he continued. "We must distinguish between his motive and that of a professional blackmailer. Howell is driven by an evil and merciless love of money and power. Westburton more despises money than craves it. As to gaining power over someone, rather than mastery he is seeking a form of servitude to Enid Westburton. I have never loved, but if I did, Watson, and if the woman I loved underwent a metamorphosis of the order Westburton swears his wife underwent in Peru, I might act even as our lawless barrister has. Men have been driven to distraction by far lesser souls. Think how the Achaeans waged war against Troy when Paris stole Helen from Menelaus. One day we might even see a King forsake the throne of England for such an *inamorata*."

Holmes leaned back on the settee, little wavering rings of smoke rising up to the ceiling, before continuing. "I expect His Majesty to arrive here at any minute. Half-an-hour ago I sent word to him at the Langham, absolving Westburton of any involvement. I assured him that he can empty the hotel safe of his fortune in uncut white diamonds and the assorted Columbian emeralds and return home."

"Holmes," I returned impatiently, "make yourself plain. Do you plan to let Westburton go scot-free?"

"Not quite," came the response. "In any case, the decision must appear to be our client's idea."

He tapped his jacket pocket. "I have Westburton's confession in writing, plus his sworn word that he'll leave our shores for good and settle in a land where he has every prospect of making the income he believes he needs to keep Enid Westburton at his side."

"Which is where?" I asked.

"Where else," came the reply, "but in the most litigious country on Earth – America – and in its most litigious city – Chicago. He'll try to wean 'Liana Monte' off her extravagant expectations and persuade her to join him, magically returned to life from the vasty deep."

"Starting anew in America?" I asked, astonished. "How can Westburton afford it?"

The reply came with an airy wave of the old briar. "Inspector Gregson persuaded Bonham's to offer our barrister friend a very substantial sum for Umiña. It'll give Bonham's excellent publicity on permanent display in Scotland Yard's Black Museum, alongside the various other items used for giving police officers practical instruction on how to detect and prevent crime."

At Holmes spoke the words "Black Museum", the rumble of a carriage drawing up outside our lodgings came through the open window.

It took twenty minutes and a pot of Mrs. Hudson's hearty black tea for Holmes to explain every detail to a rapt King. Our Royal visitor's eyes sparkled. He sent up a blue triumphant cloud from his cigarette and gave Holmes a penetrating stare, "but - *Was ist zu tun mit* Westburton?"

"Your Majesty," Holmes replied gravely, "his fate lies entirely in your hands. He waits trembling at his temporary lodgings for news of your decision. He knows we have sufficient evidence to strip him of membership in the Bar and the Honourable Society of the Inner Temple and to put him on trial where he, for a change, must take the stand."

The King's brow clouded. "A public trial before a gallery packed to the brim by reporters from the sensational press," he muttered. "That could have unfortunate consequences for me."

Holmes responded, "Your Majesty, perhaps you might offer Westburton a way out instead?"

"For example, Holmes?" the King asked, a keen look crossing his face.

"You can demand a signed confession and a promise to leave England at once, never to return."

"I agree," the King accepted hastily. "Yes, that's it! Gentlemen, let him know I will take nothing less than a full confession and a solemn promise to leave England, never to return. That will do. It's punishment enough. Once you have obtained both, I'm inclined to show magnanimity – even to get a regular remittance to him. In fact, from the very start I considered this attempt at extortion quite entertaining."

Sotto voce, Holmes muttered, "Watson, so much for the 'Iron Fist'."

To the King he said, "A wise and generous offer, Your Majesty. I'm sure he'll accept those terms and abide by them. There's no more to be done in the matter except for a settlement of our expenses and my fee, after which Watson and I shall have the honour to wish you a very good journey home."

"But what of Howell?" the King asked suddenly.

"That's something, alas, beyond our powers, Your Majesty. I'm afraid there's nothing we can do about him within the Law. Howell will get away scot-free. *Latet anguis in herba*."

Our visitor rose. The hang-dog look of recent days had vanished. He strode across to the hat stand. From his cloak he took a bulging pouch. It tinkled merrily as he dropped it on the breakfast table.

"Gentlemen," he said, with a bow, "you may gather from the sum in gold in this purse precisely how appreciative I am."

At this he turned to Holmes and grasped him by the shoulders. "Mr. Holmes, there is one last ceremony I wish to perform." The King reached into a second pocket and extricated the small gold box. "We shall have it engraved right away on Regent's Street."

As he spoke, the screech of a carriage wheel scraping the kerb came up from the street, followed by the thumping of feet coming up the stairs two or three at a time. The door crashed open. Inspector Gregson rushed into the room.

"Mr. Holmes," he called out breathlessly, "what is it? Why the urgent summons? Has someone been murdered – ?"

The police officer caught sight of our guest. "Your Majesty," Gregson exclaimed, throwing a sideways look at Holmes with a questioning and rather startled gaze, uncertain whether he should suppress any mention of his own involvement in the case, "I had no idea – "

"Of course you didn't, Gregson," Holmes assured him cheerily. "It's all highly confidential. His Majesty is here solely because he has an official duty to perform before he returns to his throne. For special services, His Majesty insists on conferring upon you, Tobias Gregson, Scotland Yard Inspector, the Freedom of his Capital city!"

Epilogue

Throughout time, blackmail has been high on the list of the foulest of crimes – cold-blooded in its premeditation and repeated in its torture of the victim. Not one woman or man in a thousand will march off to the Chief Magistrate at Bow Street to make a sworn statement detailing all that they know about the extortioner. Howell's access to the closed and privileged *milieu* of Aristocracy continued, with scandalous gossip its everyday currency. It was of some small satisfaction to us that Howell's involvement in this matter failed to gain him even one krona, let alone a share of raw diamonds or the uncut emeralds the extortion letter demanded. The king of blackmailers continued to be known as the pit-viper *fer-de-lance*. More than half of the victims he sank his fangs into ended up killing themselves while he waxed richer and richer.

One night in April 1890 his nemesis struck. A piece appeared in the weekly magazine *Tit-Bits* announcing his death in circumstances as strange as any Poe or Ainsworth novel. The butler at Tilney Street reported his master had failed to return home. A corpse identified as Charles Augustus Howell, fine art dealer, was found near a Chelsea public house, an area known for ribaldry and flaunting vice. At first it was assumed he was the victim of a common street robbery except for the fact the pavement was curiously lacking in pools of blood, indicating his death had taken place elsewhere. A *post mortem* examination found the throat had been slit posthumously, slashed with such venom that the windpipe was sliced right through and the head nearly severed. The presence of a half-sovereign coin left with a victim's body was known to be a criticism of those guilty of slander. In this instance, what went unreported was there was also, jutting from the oozing wound, a curious addition to the gold coin – a gilded bronze key, the splendid rank-insignia of the Grand Chamberlain of The Councils of Scandinavia.

Knowing Holmes's general commitment to due process, no matter how disgraceful the crime, I tried to draw my comrade-in-arms into expressing a view on such extreme savagery inflicted without legal proceeding, almost certainly by cohorts of the King. Holmes declined to answer, though for several days he seemed unusually at peace with the world.

***

My comrade Sherlock Holmes maintained a prudent discretion over detail of such delicate cases. I was later to record another commission, that time concerning an English milord.

Lord St. Simon: *"A most painful matter to me, as you can most readily imagine, Mr. Holmes. I have been cut to the quick. I understand that you have already managed several delicate cases of this sort, sir, though I presume that they were hardly from the same class of society."*

Sherlock Holmes: "No, I am descending."

"I beg pardon."

"My last client of the sort was a king."

"Oh, really! I had no idea. And which king?"

"The King of Scandinavia."

"What! Had he lost his wife?"

"You can understand," said Holmes suavely, "that I extend to the affairs of my other clients the same secrecy which I promise to you in yours."

– Lord St. Simon and Sherlock Holmes
'*The Adventure of the Noble Bachelor*'

The End

NOTES

Surnames. Holmes's and Watson's use of each other's surnames surprises today's readers. In the twenty-first century, even in Britain, it seems strange that very good friends in past times used each other's family names in the way we would now use a first name. No character in the original Sherlock Holmes stories except Holmes's older brother Mycroft ever called him "Sherlock", nor did anyone call Watson "John", (except presumably his wife Mary). The use of the surname/family name was considered both correct and friendly among British schoolboys and among adults alike.

Urvogel. 'First bird.' Watson refers to Archaeopteryx (A. lithographica), the fossils of which are synonymous with the Solnhofen quarries and dug up in 1861. Watson must have been reading about it. However, Archaeopteryx was probably not the first bird to evolve.

The Langham. The hotel was mentioned in three Sherlock Holmes stories: Captain Morstan – Watson's father-in-law - was staying there in 'The Sign of Four'; the King of Bohemia holed up there while in London in 'A Scandal in Bohemia'; and the Hon. Philip Green gave the Langham as his London address in 'The Disappearance of Lady Frances Carfax'.

Eisenfaust. The Iron Fist. The King knows Holmes speaks fluent German.

Canoe Landau. An elegant (and costly) all-weather day-and-night coach so-named from its curved body. The carriage was developed in Landau, Germany, in the mid-18th century.

Bishop Colenso. "I have myself just returned from Cape Colony. I have no doubt that you are tolerant of Zulu polygamy! Clearly you are a heretical follower of Bishop Colenso!" shouts Holmes at the hapless Vicar of St. Catherine's. The real Bishop Colenso, John William Colenso (1814 – 1883), was a Cornish cleric and defender of Zulu traditions who served as the first Bishop of Natal. Colenso had courted controversy with the publication in 1855 of his 'Remarks on the Proper Treatment of Polygamy', one of the most cogent Christian-based arguments for tolerance of the Zulu custom for men to marry many spouses.

Oscar Gustaf Rejlander. From The Victorian Web. The photographer Oscar Gustaf Rejlander (1813-1875) was born in Stockholm. Described as "an English portrait photographer of Swedish origin", he became Julia Cameron's favourite photographer, while Lewis Carroll, another friend and admirer, found some "very beautiful" prints and negatives among his collection when he visited the studio. Carroll later bought some of the prints for his own collection.

Blackmail. Amazingly, blackmail did not become a criminal offence in England until the Theft Act of 1968. Blackmail is defined under English criminal law as an unwarranted demand with menaces, with a view to making a gain or causing a loss. Menaces can include a threat of physical violence, but other forms – such as a threat to expose a secret – can constitute blackmail.

Defuncti sunt. 'They are dead.' Watson's Latin was competent from his schooling and medical training.

Elysian. From the idyllic Greek mythological place called Elysian Fields.

Fer-de-Lance. Pit-viper. One of the world's most deadly snakes. Its haemotoxic venom spreads through cells and blood vessels, causing swelling and blisters and destroying tissue. In the lowlands of Central America, it can reach lengths of up to six feet and is responsible for more than half of all venomous bites.

Gasogene Bottle. Late Victorian device for producing carbonated water.

Latet anguis in herba - '*The snake lurks in the grass*.' A treacherous person. Holmes showing that he knew unusual Latin phrases. First known use by the poet Virgil.

Umiña To the Inca of Peru, emeralds symbolised the tears of the moon goddess. Garcilasso the Inca was the son of an army captain and an Incan princess. He wrote of a legendary emerald bearing the name of Umiña, almost as large as an ostrich egg, worshipped by the people of Manta.

The Case of the Impressionist Painting

Chapter I

A Prospective Client Arrives

I was alone at 221B, Baker Street. Holmes had yet to return from a clandestine visit to the Royal Albert Dock, this time disguised as a tramp. I wondered whether to remind our housekeeper Mrs. Hudson of her recent generous offer to pull a bottle of Hochheim's Königin Victoriaberg from her 'wine cellar' (the coal room), gifted to her twenty years earlier. She would, she said, uncork the bottle in a few days' time when Sherlock Holmes and I celebrated our first year as co-lodgers. Those were early days in his career when he was still building his reputation, when cases arrived which were to make him the most famous private consulting detective in Europe.

Mrs. Hudson came up the stairs. "There's a gentleman at the front door," she said, handing me a calling card. "He insists on seeing Mr. Holmes." The card read '*William Henry Perrin, Fellow Royal Chemistry Society, Proprietor Perrin Dyeworks*'. I asked her to see him up.

A man of a pleasant but troubled demeanour entered the sitting room. Before I could introduce myself, he grasped my hand and exclaimed, "Mr. Holmes, it's extremely good of you to – "

I interrupted, smiling. "I'm Dr. John Watson, Mr. Holmes's co-lodger. He'll be returning shortly. Meantime," I added, "do sit down and tell me the purpose of your visit."

He looked reticent. I said, "You may be absolutely frank with me, Mr. Perrin." I took his valise and invited him to hang his tailored velvet opera cape on the coat rack. The lavender silk lining matched the colour of his bow tie.

We settled into the comfortable chairs by the fireside. My visitor offered a heartfelt, "Dr. Watson, you invite me to be frank. I have no need to tell you my presence here indicates my situation is bleak. I presume we can agree that being blackmailed is a desperate situation! Blackmailed by a fiend!"

He then related how some twenty-five years earlier he'd been a student of chemistry at the Royal College where he made a chance discovery. From a derivative of coal-tar he produced the most wonderful light-purple dye now universally known as *mauveine*, or Florentine Mallow. The colour became the height of fashion among the *beau monde* of Paris and London – so much so the frenzy it inspired became known as "mauveine measles". Queen Victoria appeared at the 1862 International Exhibition wearing a silk dress coloured by his dye. In France, Empress Eugenie, wife of Napoleon III, and her ladies-in-waiting wore mauveine-dyed dresses to state functions.

Restless, he stood up and crossed to the windows to peer down at the street. “That opera cape, Dr. Watson,” he clarified over his shoulder. “I’m a man of considerable wealth but not a patron of the Arts. I had it specially made for my visit here today, aiming to throw anyone off the scent. I booked a seat for the matinee at the Opera House and walked straight through the building to the stage entrance at the far side, to be certain I was not being followed.”

He bent down to withdraw a thin sheaf of documents from the valise.

“Being able to speak freely after three weeks during which I have trusted no one will be a considerable relief. You are a doctor of – ?”

“Medicine,” I replied. “Until last year a surgeon attached to the 66th Berkshire Regiment of Foot in Afghanistan.”

I gestured at the sheaf of papers. “But do continue, please,” I added.

He began to describe the parlous situation which had brought him to our Baker Street sitting room, handing me a telegraph.

“It started when that arrived.”

In capital letters it read - *IN MEMORIAM R.M. OBIIT MDCCCLXXXI.*

“*R.M.*?” I enquired.

“Robert Miller. I was surprised,” he continued, “because I wasn’t aware Robert had died in an accident.”

He explained Miller had been the owner of a large dye works in Mill Street, Perth, a remarkable chemist in his own right.

“I first reached out to him years ago, when I was a student at the Royal College, studying under Dr. August von Hofmann, a pioneer in the chemistry of carbon-based molecules, and specifically chemicals being isolated from coal-tar. Dr. von Hofmann encouraged me to seek a natural alkaloid substitute for quinine, for the treatment of some forms of malaria. Doubtless you know from your time in the Far East that the world is critically short of medication for malaria parasites. I decided to start by oxidising allyl toluidine."

Quinine was derived from the bark of the cinchona tree, grown mainly in South America. Its cost was exorbitant, and the supply far short of the amount needed for the vast number of malaria cases. I said I could only imagine the formidable task ahead of a chemist who ventured into quinine synthesis. "The development of synthetic quinine would be a milestone in organic chemistry," I stated, "but I don't recall reading about any such discovery."

"For good reason," my guest replied wryly. "Oxidising allyl toluidine was a route doomed to failure from the start. I tried formulation after formulation. No quinine was formed – only a dirty reddish-brown precipitate."

"So what made you communicate with the proprietor of a dye-works?" I queried. "It's quite a leap from looking for an artificial remedy for plasmodium parasites to entering the field of dye-making."

"As you say," Perrin agreed, "but I sought Robert's advice for good reason. As I explained earlier, during my coal-tar experiments I chanced upon a rare form of purple dye. I wanted to know if the dye might have any commercial possibilities. If so, should I apply for a patent?"

"Ah," I said, smiling, "Kismet! What are the chances of experimenting with coal-tar derivatives for a quinine substitute and by chance discovering…"

For the first time a glimmer of a smile crossed my visitor's face.

"Am I to understand you believe in Fate, Dr. Watson?" He added impishly, "A result of too long spent in the mystic East, perhaps?"

"No and yes," I replied. "No I do not, because it's irrational. Yes I do, because otherwise I cannot properly divine how I came to meet Sherlock Holmes a few days short of one year ago."

I retold how I'd planned to live out my professional life as an Army surgeon, until Fate decided otherwise. A Jezail bullet shattered my shoulder at the Battle of Maiwand. Overnight, I became a discarded pawn, a forgotten element in 'The Great Game' played out between St. Petersburg and London for supremacy in Central Asia.

Had the damage not been so serious, I would never have returned to England so precipitously. Then once more Fate stepped in, this time at Piccadilly Circus. I was standing at the Criterion Bar when someone tapped me on the shoulder. Turning round I recognised young Stamford, my former orderly at Barts. Later that fateful day Stamford introduced me to a person also in need of someone to help share the expenses of bachelor's quarters. The man's name was Sherlock Holmes.

"Then Destiny must have two faces," my visitor replied, "like the Roman deity, Janus. One looking forward, one looking backward. I've done well in the world of chemistry," he added, "yet now I sit here awaiting the arrival of a private consulting detective, to beg him to save me from a blackmailer intent on murdering my very soul!"

At this he broke down. Pitifully he cried out, "What have I done to bring this about?"

The sound of the front door opening and banging shut was followed by Holmes's familiar footsteps taking the stairs two at a time. Perrin and I got to our feet and turned to greet him.

Holmes shook hands with our visitor in a business-like manner and waved him back to the chair by the grate. I handed over the telegraph concerning the passing of Robert Miller and gave a synopsis from my notes of my conversation with Perrin.

"Mr. Perrin," my comrade continued, "first may I say that to those of us with a particular interest in chemistry, your fame goes before you."

Holmes motioned towards his chemical table in the corner of the sitting room.

"Dr. Watson will tell you that I myself experiment with coal-tar derivatives. But please go on."

Perrin's worried expression returned.

He resumed, "Soon afterwards, I received a second communication, a cutting from *The Perthshire Constitutional and Journal*. I'll read it to you."

> *It has been revealed that during the very early hours of the morning a* cluinntinn mèirleach *(phantom thief) entered the premises of the North British Dyeworks, formerly J. Miller and Sons Ltd., on North Street, Perth. The office filing cabinets were jemmied open and some files removed. A nearby safe known to contain a large amount of money for the weekly wages was not broken into. Consequently, it seems the thieves may have lost their nerve and left with nothing of value.*

Perrin looked up.

"The break-in must have taken place just an hour after poor Robert's death."

Holmes asked, "Did you have any idea why this was sent?"

Perrin replied, "At the time, no."

Again he reached into the valise.

"A week passed and I received this letter. It bears no signature and as you can see, it was produced on a typewriter."

Dear Mr. Perrin,

The Perthshire Constitutional and Journal *was misguided in saying nothing of value was taken. Files dated to 1856 concerning the discovery of an interesting new purple dye were removed. The drawer contained a wonderful mauve bow-tie (enclosed) and extensive correspondence between you and the lamentably deceased Robert Miller, also taken.*

"This can't be the last communication," I said, puzzled. "While they've been odd, so far I see no sign of blackmail."

"It wasn't the last," Perrin confirmed, passing over an envelope. "This came only a day or two later. It contains a letter in Robert Miller's own hand, meant to seem as if written many years ago in reply to my very first letter to him."

I asked, "The earlier reference to '*the lamentably deceased Robert Miller*' – why did the writer use the word '*lamentably*'?"

"The fact Robert died is lamentable enough, but the circumstances of his death were doubly lamentable. He always worked late at the factory, but one night he worked even later. The weather was inclement. He beckoned a cab waiting for custom on the other side of the road. He was crossing to get into it when the horses bolted straight at him. Before Robert could save himself, he was under the horses' hooves and died within the hour. The cabbie was never traced."

"There was nobody else in the street?" asked Holmes.

"Just a passer-by walking a dog. He had noticed the cab, a heavy coach pulled by four horses. He hadn't seen one plying for trade that late before. He said the horses took off as if they'd been raced – as though trained to bolt out of a starting gate."

"Did this witness give any details of the carriage?" Holmes asked.

"It was too dark for him to make out the driver or a cab plate but the passer-by must have had some knowledge of the equine world. He said the four-in-hand were American Quarter Horses, an unusual breed for a hackney carriage," Perrin replied.

I opened the envelope and took out a vellum sheet. The heading was that of the dye works in Perth. It was signed '*Robert Miller*' and dated more than two decades earlier.

Dear Mr. Perrin,

Thank you for the letter of the 5th instant regarding your chemical experiments with coal-tar derivatives. You say your initial experimentation to discover an artificial alternative to quinine failed, but you believe there could be a particular colourful dye inherent in the derivatives. As the owner of dye works, I can be of considerable help regarding aniline dyes. I have been experimenting in such matters for some time now, for commercial purposes, especially in the light-purple range. My works have recently received a Royal Warrant from Her Majesty, and we refer to ourselves as silk dye makers to the Queen.

You report that your efforts resulted only in a reddish powder and an oily pitch-black substance, rather than the glistening white crystals of quinine. I had similar results in my search for a new dye, but by persevering I have recently made a break-through by introducing alcohol into my experimentation. I have discovered an entirely new way to produce a colour very similar to the flower of the Mallow plant. For some two thousand years, a major colourant in this spectrum has been Tyrian Purple, obtained at immense cost from Murex brandaris *and* Murex trunculus. *It took thousands of the molluscs to dye one toga – such a rarity that Julius Caesar decreed the colour could only be worn by Roman emperors and their families.*

The new dye has proved fast on silk. Regarding its commercial possibilities, it is vital that it also be fast on cotton, an immensely larger and more challenging market. If it is, it will be worth my company's while to apply for a patent.

I admire your enthusiasm. These are wonderful times for the advancement of chemistry. Being eighteen, as you say you are, you are at the right age to take advantage to the full. May I suggest you come to Perth to discuss whether you should take leave of the Royal College and assist me in my work on the cotton challenge and in my preparation of a patent application? I shall be delighted to cover all your expenses.

Yours very sincerely,
Robert Miller, Proprietor

I remarked, "A very pleasant letter."

Our visitor looked at me with a strange expression.

"Very pleasant indeed, Dr. Watson," he acknowledged, "but I don't think one syllable of it was composed by Robert. I had never had sight of it until it was delivered to my home in the early hours a fortnight ago. Despite the date on it, the content convinces me it could only have been counterfeited following the theft of those files."

I started to ask, "Then why would anyone compose such a remarkably welcoming – ?"

"*Gentlemen, Gentlemen*!" Perrin broke in impatiently, "if you read it as I read it, it makes out with devilish cunning and in no uncertain terms that Robert, not I, discovered mauveine, that I stole the credit, and worse, that I knavishly patented the dye in my name. That artful letter prepared me for the worst – and then this came."

He brought out a further piece of paper.

"This arrived yesterday – typed, as you see. Especially note the post-script."

I read out, '*I suggest we meet soonest,* en-plein-air, *and forestall any difficulties which may arise between us. The Capital would be fine. Place an advertisement in* The Evening Standard. *State a precise place, date, time.*'

The post-script added, '*It strikes me that the Royal Chemistry Society might find the Miller letter of great historical value for their annals, don't you agree?*'

"It came with these two cuttings from *The Illustrated London News*," Perrin continued, "enclosures so idiosyncratic, so odd, I assume they were included by mistake. What bearing they have on any matter of concern to me is unfathomable."

I took them from him. The first indicated that Christie's was holding an auction. '*A great sale of pictures, sculpture, Sevres, Dresden, Chinese, and Japanese porcelain, decorative furniture, bronzes, and works of ornamental art and fine materials, brought from a Duke's Palace.*'

The first excerpt was followed by a second. '*A painting of especial interest. Portrait of Philip IV of Spain, which was taken from the Palace at Madrid during the Peninsular War by the French General Dessolle, from whose family it found its way to the Estate of the Duke. It is one of the finest portraits by Valasquez.*'

It concluded with '*An anonymous bid of six thousand guineas has already been submitted.*'

I pointed out to Holmes the final sentence was doubly underlined in red ink.

"Good Lord!" I continued. "Six thousand guineas! It's astonishing to think any painting could be worth as much as a fine house in Belgravia!"

I pointed at the newly framed portrait of General "China" Gordon on the wall of the sitting room. "I paid only twenty guineas for that, including the cost of the frame."

"When did the auction take place?" Holmes asked.

"It hasn't yet," I replied, looking at the cuttings. "It's in a few days' time."

"Mr. Perrin," Holmes asked, lighting his pipe, "was it you who underlined that last sentence?"

"It was not," came the response.

"Then we must presume the blackmailer is the anonymous bidder," Holmes continued. "He will be calling on you to provide him with the six thousand guineas to secure the Velasquez portrait."

In a voice breaking with despair, Perrin wailed, "Money I have, but payment would be an admission of guilt – what would stop this vampire leeching and leeching, and then deciding through some malevolence of mind to send that forgery of a letter to the Royal Chemistry Society anyway! With Robert's death and the evidence stolen from the factory cabinet, I have nothing to disprove the calumnies implied in it. My career and reputation will be at an end."

I asked, "The patent in question, did Mr. Miller ever take one out?"

"Not on mauveine," came the reply. "He was perfectly aware I alone had made the discovery. I even sent him the once-white bow-tie I'm wearing today, returned to me by the blackmailer. I had plunged it into my dye. As you can see, it turned the white silk into a wonderful pale violet."

"How close is the writing to Robert Miller's own?" Holmes asked. "The shape and slope of the letters, regularity of the spacing?"

"A specialist in handwriting has checked it for me. He could not find one jot of difference," came the unhappy response.

"Blackmailers can be seen off, Mr. Perrin," I remarked. "A book printer threatened to publish a salacious memoir by a former mistress of the great Duke of Wellington. It was made clear only money – in copious amounts – could keep his name out of those red-hot pages. Wellington sent the letter back with a message scrawled across it, '*Publish and be damned!*' Why not emulate the Duke?"

"Doctor," Perrin returned morosely, "were I the Iron Duke, I would reply in exactly those terms. His hard-won reputation as the conqueror of Napoleon was hardly at stake. Besides, half the aristocracy of Great Britain and even the eldest son of our Great Queen indulge in such affairs."

At this he clambered out of his chair and strode to the door leading to the landing. He thrust it open, checking for listeners, before closing it and returning to us. He withdrew a sheaf of telegrams from a pocket.

"Look at these, gentlemen. They will impress upon you the seriousness of my predicament. La Société Chimique de Paris is considering offering me their most prestigious medal. It will mean tens of thousands of pounds – possibly hundreds of thousands – in further revenue for my factories. The Technische Hochschule of Munich is offering me an Honorary Doctorate. So too is the University of Leiden, and also my alma mater Würzburg. As to America, I am invited to make a tour – New York, Chicago, San Francisco! If that letter goes to The Royal Chemistry Society, all and sundry will consider me a plagiariser, a counterfeiter, a forger, a copier, a cheat, an impostor, a cribber.

"I shall no longer hear a word from any of them. Every such offer already made will be withdrawn, every likely offer of awards nipped in the bud, such is the suspicion this wretched letter will instill in their minds. Seven years ago, the Royal Society awarded me the Copley Medal for my numerous contributions to the science of chemistry. It will be taken from me, together with the Royal Medal. They may even strip me of my Fellowship. I shall no longer be welcomed by Her Majesty and the Prince Consort at the Palace.

"I tell you, Mr. Holmes and Dr. Watson, before you stands a desperate man. This is no ordinary blackmailer. He has the mind of a king cobra. All my wealth is as nothing when I consider how bleak my life will become if this criminal is allowed to proceed at will. You must fend him off. Trounce him. Otherwise, not one person in all England with means and reputation will be safe."

"Then, sir, we must start right away," Holmes ordered. "Place the advertisement in *The Evening Standard* exactly as he asks. He is hoist with the petard of passion to possess the Velasquez. There could be opportunity in that. He'll want to impress upon you precisely how well his plan has been prepared to your extreme disadvantage, as indeed it has. I don't doubt the scheme was long in gestation. If his case appears strong, you must tell him you will pay, but add you'll need several days to put the vast sum together without others taking note. By then we may have a chance to discover his identity. Mr. Perrin, I must warn you, Dr. Watson and I can offer no guarantee. As you say, this is no ordinary criminal. He displays cunning, the like of which I've never encountered."

I saw our new client down to the street. As he entered a cab he looked out at me.

"Dr. Watson," he asserted bravely. "You have given me courage. I shall try to muster enough to stand up to this snake of a human being."

"Good man!" I called back.

Holmes was still in his position by the window when I returned. I gave a questioning look.

"What do you make of it all?" I asked. "I take it you've had quite some experience of blackmailers?"

He shook his head.

"None."

He crossed the room to knock out his pipe in the grate.

"Blackmail is a curious crime, a common object of criminal prohibition, the ugliest of transgressions. It's rightly said that when a portion of wealth passes out of the hands of him who has acquired it without his consent, whether by force or by artifice, to him who hasn't created it, property is violated, plunder perpetrated – yet it can be paradoxical. Take the Miller letter. On one reading it threatens Perrin – pay up or your reputation in the world of chemistry will be put in extreme danger. Yet on another reading it could be taken as a demand for justice for the unfortunate Robert Miller, deceased."

With an unexpected change of subject, Holmes asked, "You had horses out in India, didn't you?"

"I did," I replied. "Two Walers. Wonderful breed."

That evening we dined at Simpson's, a ritual we practiced whenever we took on a new client. Holmes chose the steamed steak-and-kidney pie. I preferred the hand-dived Scottish scallops. Both of us decided on a dessert of vanilla, cinnamon, cream, and bitter and sweet almonds.

Two days later I left our lodgings and went to the one-legged news-vendor at the Baker Street Station to purchase *The Evening Standard*. I turned to the personal ads. The first one read '*CAD: Utterly miserable and broken-hearted. I must see you my darling. Please write and fix time and place, at all risks. Can pass house if necessary unseen, in close carriage.*'

Starkly, the next personal ad read '*Tomorrow Highgate Cemetery one p.m. Grave of Alfred Swaine Taylor.*'

I took the newspaper home. Holmes was at his chemical table. The sitting room was filled with acrid fumes. I told him, "A meeting is set for tomorrow at Alfred Swaine Taylor's grave. It must be Perrin's advertisement. Taylor was a chemist, wasn't he?"

"He was," Holmes replied. "Author of *On Poisoning by Strychnia*. I attended his funeral. His grave lies near a very grand mausoleum, that of a Julius Beer."

Chapter II

A Fraught Encounter in Highgate Cemetery

At around a quarter-past-two the following day, Holmes and I were in a cab being pulled up the steep hill to Highgate Cemetery. We paid off the driver and took a side-path to the Circle of Lebanon, the most circumspect way to reach Alfred Swaine Taylor's grave. The Cemetery was a fashionable place to bequeath one's corpse to the soil. Lower down, a combination of coal-fired stoves and poor sanitation made the air heavy and foul-smelling. By contrast, the air of Highgate was fresh. Flowers and trees grew well. The labyrinth of Egyptian sepulchres, Gothic tombs, and a litany of silent stone angels were safe from extremes of pitting and weathering.

At the heart of the Circle was a Biblical 'First of Trees', a massive cedar which towered over the landscape like a huge bonsai, the base surrounded by a circle of tombs. We paused under its graceful branches to survey the route ahead. Holmes pointed across a patchwork of toppled gravestones and grandiose mausolea to where a man was standing at an easel.

“Where the artist’s at work,” he said, “that’s the Julius Beer Mausoleum. Taylor’s grave is close by. In fact,” he added, “look over there. There’s our client.”

Perrin was slumped down. He had been scribbling notes. He looked utterly woebegone. On seeing us he cried out, “It’s no use, Holmes. Unless I pay whatever he demands and for as long as he demands, I am lost. The man’s the Devil – the Devil incarnate!”

“So the blackmailer arrived?” I prompted solicitously.

Perrin paled.

“He did,” came the reply.

“And?” I prompted.

“He congratulated me on my cranium. He told me I have a marked ‘patch of wonder’ – hence my inventive ability.”

I said, “I presume he then – ?”

“He did. He told me he was here solely to impress on me why I should hand over six thousand guineas in not more than three days.”

“Conveniently in time for the auction of the Velasquez,” I said.

“His age?” Holmes asked.

“About mine,” Perrin estimate. “I’d hazard over forty. Perhaps forty-five.”

“Height?” I prompted

“That was notable,” Perrin replied. “Very tall, accentuated by being thin.”

“The face?” I asked.

“Even more notable – the forehead especially. It domed out in a white curve. Eyes deeply sunken for a man of his relative youth. The shoulders rounded, as though from much study.”

He paused, reflecting. With a shudder he burst out, “Then he began to speak. Every sneer was a hammer-blow. I was writing notes when you arrived but I hardly need them. His words will remain etched into my brain for the rest of my life. He addressed me as "My dear Perrin". Then he went on, saying, "You and I are here for the sole purpose of deciding whether you should hand over a considerable amount of money – six thousand guineas, in fact. I am here to convince you that you should. I suggest our business together will be done faster if I start first, to convince you a refusal will have the most deleterious effect on your well-being".

He went on, "On the one hand, we can agree a time for you to return here within three days with such a sum. On the other, you can refuse, and the Miller letter will be delivered to the Royal Chemistry Society. In my private life I am a man of standing. If by chance you discover my identity and report matters to Scotland Yard, and were I consequently to be placed in the dock, I would convince judge and jury that I'm a humble citizen who chanced across a letter, a letter establishing it was the late Robert Miller, not you, who came across Florentine Mallow in doing his own scientific experiments with coal-tar derivatives. By contrast, I would point out your experiments under Dr. von Hofmann were seeking a substitute for quinine, but quinine is achromatic. It has no colourant properties whatsoever. It wouldn't turn silk or cotton purple.

"The letter proves it was Miller who determined a purple dye could be derived from coal-tar. He had the factory and the financial capacity to conduct every experiment imaginable. Even if by chance you had come across the dye at that stage, your laboratory was a hut in your back garden. Further, I would put it to the Court the letter shows it wasn't you but Miller who planned to apply for a patent, but you cheated him out of it through your deplorable opportunism."

Perrin produced a handkerchief and wiped his brow. I offered him a gulp of restorative liquor.

"Mr. Holmes, he is a man of implacable evil who has done his research formidably well. Back than I was a mere eighteen years of age. A jury wouldn't believe I alone carried out the experiments leading to the discovery and soon the patenting of Florentine Mallow, although that's the truth of it. Plainly they would take the blackmailer's side – that I stole the formula and patented it in my name."

"On what terms did you part?" I asked.

"He said I should return here on Saturday at the same hour, bringing the money," Perrin cried out. "I can see no way out but to comply with his demand."

"We have three days," Holmes murmured. "Watson, we must allow our client to wend his way home."

Perrin shook our hands. Despite the cold his face glistened with sweat. He started towards the path leading to the great cedar of Lebanon and the exit beyond. After a yard or two he halted.

"Mr. Holmes," he called back in a voice which shook as though his oppressor was still present, "there was something …something about him, like a predatory reptile of the order *Crocodilia*. When he turned his back on me, I expected to see a row of spines sprouting from the nape of his neck to the tip of a tail."

We stood watching his departure.

"We can be sure of one thing," Holmes muttered. "If we fail, it won't be solely Perrin's reputation the press and public will shred like Savoy cabbage."

The path took us back towards the Julius Beer Mausoleum. The artist was still there, dabbing at a convincing watercolour. My comrade left my side and stepped across to him and asked, "Did you get it?" The artist pulled out a charcoal sketch from under the canvas. A face leered out, the forehead white and domed, the eyes deeply sunken, the shoulders hunched, exactly as Perrin had described his tormentor.

"Take it to Scotland Yard immediately," Holmes ordered the artist, handing over three guineas. "Ask for Inspector Lestrade. Tell him Sherlock Holmes should be glad of any information which could help identify this man. Inform Lestrade we need to discover who he is before Saturday. Make it clear his likeness must not appear in any newspaper. This is not a missing person or an unidentified corpse."

The following morning Holmes joined me at the fireside as I caught up with the Court and Social page of *The Times*. We began to sort through the first post of the morning when a banging came at the street door. This was followed by the sound of a visitor greeting Mrs. Hudson in familiar terms before hurrying up the stairs to our sitting room, chortling loudly. It was Inspector Lestrade.

"Gentlemen!" he cried out, waving the depiction of the man who had so terrified our client at Highgate Cemetery. "I circulated this around the Yard. There was nothing remotely like him in our files. We seemed on a hiding to nothing regarding his identity." He shed his coat. "However, by chance we have discovered his identity – except we can't possibly have the right man. He can't be your blackmailer, Mr. Holmes!"

The inspector's eyes sparkled as he spoke. He was evidently in a state of barely-suppressed exultation. He slapped the drawing with the back of his hand.

"This man was recognised by a constable who joined us after deciding not to pursue the priesthood at Hackney College – the Divinity school. He's certain it's the man who taught him philosophy and astronomy, a Professor O'Clery. If you're seeking a ruthless, cunning, and decisively malicious person, it can't be O'Clery. His career has been spent among seminarians preparing for life in the Church."

He looked from one to the other of us to gauge our reaction. I was about to say this wasn't the most welcome piece of news we had ever received when Holmes asked, "How long ago was this constable at the College?"

Lestrade looked at the paper in his hand.

"He left four years ago, but the Professor's still there. My constable was on a return visit to his old academic haunt the other day and spotted him crossing a courtyard."

"He's quite certain the sketch identifies O'Clery?" I asked.

"Adamant! The seminars were held in the Professor's study. Our constable remembers them well. If a seminar got boring, my man would spend the time gazing at an oil-painting above the mantelpiece – a copy of a beach scene in France, he said."

Holmes asked, "Did your constable learn the name of the artist who painted the original?"

"A Frog – " Lestrade checked back with his notes. "– by the name of Claude Monet."

"The title?" Holmes asked.

"Holmes, for heaven's sake!" I cried out in exasperation. "The inspector has work to do, yet you keep him here discussing a painting! This Professor O'Clery can't be our man! What does it matter what it was called – or who painted the original?"

"The title of the painting, Lestrade?" Holmes repeated. "Did the constable recollect the title?"

"As a matter of fact he did, Mr. Holmes," Lestrade replied, addressing his notes again. "The original was titled 'La Plage de Trouville'. On one occasion, waiting until all the students had turned up, Professor O'Clery talked about the picture. Two ladies with parasols on a sandy beach and so on. Painted ten or twelve years ago, on the Frog's honeymoon."

With nothing else to report, Lestrade turned to go. I stood up and helped him back into his coat. I thanked him and saw him down the stairs to the front door. Disconsolate, I returned to the sitting room.

"Clearly we haven't found our blackmailer," I reminded Holmes. "I'm astonished you kept Lestrade here as long as you did, going on about a copy of a Monet. It's ludicrous to suppose a professor at a seminary of all places could be the –"

Holmes interrupted my flow. "Nevertheless, tomorrow we shall pay the Theological College a visit." Then he added, "We could find the Monet very interesting." He reached for his coat. "In the meantime, I'm off to Lumber Court."

I stared after him as he headed for the door. The narrow thoroughfare at St. Giles was known only for tradesmen dealing in second- or third-hand clothes of a most varied and dilapidated kind.

Chapter III

We Take a Cab to Hackney College

The next day a cab dropped us off at the College entrance. Holmes had been in the best of spirits on our journey, prattling away about Cremona fiddles and the differences between a Stradivarius and an Amati. We were in priestly garb. Rummaging around Lumber Court the previous evening, he had come across two sets from a royal peculiar which had found their discernibly weary way to St. Giles from St. Katharine's by the Tower.

A young seminarian standing at the College entrance offered to show us to Professor O'Clery's study. He was one of his students, he informed us. Conversationally Holmes asked, "I've heard he has an interest in the French Impressionists?"

Our escort smiled.

"He has," he replied. "All of us seminarians have become very familiar with the copy of a Monet over his study mantel. Not just Impressionists, though. He could lecture on the whole of European Art, right down to the Flemish and Dutch Bamboccianti if he were so inclined – but he sticks to astronomy and philosophy."

He left us at the study entrance with a polite bow.

I knocked on the door. A voice called out "Come in!".

Professor O'Clery was precisely as portrayed in the sketch. He came towards us with a welcoming smile. As soon as we'd shaken his hand, Holmes pointed at the painting in pride of place over the mantelpiece. Conversationally he remarked, "Professor, I hear you are attracted to the French Impressionists."

"I am," came the professor's reply. "Renoir, Sisley, Bazille, but – " He gestured at the painting. " – this Monet in particular. How perfectly it captures a moment by the sea. The windswept beach. The unmediated colours. Alas, fine as it is, this isn't the original. As a humble professor on a modest seminary wage, I must make do with a copy, naturally."

"Naturally," Holmes murmured. "I believe the original was stolen and has yet to be recovered."

"So I've heard," the professor replied.

With a polite, "If I may," my comrade crossed to the painting. He lent forward, peering closely at it.

"This figure of a woman lost in thought," he remarked, "is she Camille-Léonie Doncieux, Monet's wife? And the second woman – would that be the wife of Eugène Boudin?"

"So we are told," came the reply. He added, "You seem surprisingly well-acquainted with it."

"My parents went to Trouville the once," Holmes explained. "The very summer Monet made this sketch."

A small movement of Holmes's hand caught my attention. Visible to me though concealed by his back from our host, Holmes had pressed his thumb against the canvas and was pulling it across the paint.

A moment later he took a seat.

"A most exceptional copy," he concluded.

Our host smiled.

"As you say," he responded.

To my consternation, Holmes gestured in my direction. "I have a question for my friend here," he continued. "He's been taking instruction at the National Gallery, reproducing copies of the great Masters."

He turned to me with an encouraging smile. "I recall your effort at a Raphael – Saint Catherine of Alexandria, wasn't it?"

On my occasional visits to the famous gallery I would pass huddles of copyists spending painstaking hours before the Raphaels, but not once had I been among their number.

Holmes gestured towards the Monet.

"Now," he addressed me, "if you were commissioned to copy an Impressionist, one painted *plein-air*, like this Monet for example, where would you undertake the work, if not at a gallery? Most probably an *atelier*?"

"Most probably an *atelier*, yes," I parroted, responding to his nod.

Holmes asked, smiling encouragingly. "To avoid the elements – wind, rain?"

"Precisely," I replied, bewildered by the topic.

Holmes pointed again at the Monet.

"Though surely in this case you'd want to stand at the exact spot as the artist himself on the beach in Normandy, surrounded by wet panel carrier, palette cups, French easel, paints, brushes, brush cleaning water, and all the rest of the artist's paraphernalia?"

"Only if I've been hit with a stick as heavy as a Penang-lawyer," I replied jocularly, entering with brio into a game I failed to grasp. "Outdoors would be absurd! I would in any case have to take along the original or a copy as exact as Professor O'Clery's."

To be sure I had made the point my comrade clearly wanted, I added, "Even then, how could I be sure the light would be the same?"

A short uncomfortable silence ensued. By the minute I was becoming convinced Holmes had made a hideously embarrassing mistake. Engaging me in a discussion so far removed from our reason for being there was undoubtedly a desperate resort. Our host was the very epitome of hospitality and courtesy. Regardless of the facial similarity to the drawing, in no way did O'Clery live up to William Perrin's alarming description of the malevolence the blackmailer radiated at the cemetery. Fortunately there would be limited time for small-talk before the seminarians arrived for a tutorial.

Chapter IV

The Denouement

"Now, gentlemen," Professor O'Clery commenced, "we must move on. You still have the advantage of me. I don't recall you giving me your names, nor the reason you chose to visit. I see from your dress you are from a Royal Peculiar. St George's Chapel at Windsor, perhaps? You can hardly have made your way here just to discuss the French Impressionists."

He looked over at the mantel clock.

"I have a mere five minutes left, so perhaps you can tell me how I can be of – "

In a preternaturally calm voice, Holmes broke in with, "Certainly, Professor O'Clery. Allow me to introduce my colleague. Despite his clerical apparel, this is Dr. John H. Watson. And I am Sherlock Holmes – a consulting detective."

"But your clothing – " said O'Clery. "I supposed you were here to help propagate the Gospel or to alleviate Swaziland's dire need for evangelists. But I must now suppose the two of you disguised yourselves as clerics to gain entry to the theology college. To what do I owe the honour? Are you engaged on a baffling case, murder in a vicarage, for example?"

Holmes's tone sharpened as he replied. "Professor, not murder in a vicarage. We are here to discuss your attempt at blackmail of the notable chemist, William Perrin. Your preparations have been at the level of genius, from the death of a dye-factory proprietor Robert Miller to the subsequent break-in at his factory in Perth, to the sequence of notes and clippings. Above all the forged Miller letter. You must stop as of now, you really must. Otherwise the consequences will be as injurious to your reputation, even to your freedom, as any you might inflict upon Perrin himself."

Even as I glanced at Holmes upon his use of the words "the death of a dye-factory proprietor", the professor slowly rose from his chair to his exceptional height.

"Sir, you astonish me. You astonish me!" he repeated, coming closer. "You enter my study unannounced. You call me a blackmailer – a murderer even! It's a case of mistaken identity as ever there was! My life is here, among priests and seminarians. My occupation is studying the Cosmos. I am a student of Euclidian planes and solid figures on the basis of axioms and theorems. Nevertheless," he said, now pausing quite close to Holmes, "for amusement before you go through that door, never to darken it again, let's say I *am* this blackmailer, and you are here in turn to blackmail *me*, threatening the ruination of my reputation, and even snatching away my liberty. How will you do that?"

Without directly replying, Holmes repeated, "Cease and desist immediately, Professor, or the consequences for you will be dramatic."

Holmes turned to me. "Come, Watson. I'm afraid that in the pleasure of this conversation, we are neglecting business of importance. This evening the Moravian virtuoso Norman-Neruda is playing a trio of Schumann pieces rearranged for violins and cello at the Hallé."

I was both aghast and puzzled at the abrupt turn in the conversation. Why had Holmes so brusquely revealed we had come under false pretences – even why we had come in the first place? What had he learned from our brush with the professor other than the latter was an aficionado of French Impressionists, something we already knew from the Scotland Yard constable's recollection of the Monet over the mantel?

Holmes reached for the hat in my hand, and then halted as though struck by an afterthought.

"Professor," he said, pointing at the painting. "One other thing. I believe I mentioned my mother and father spent that one summer in Trouville."

"I believe you did, Mr. Holmes," the professor answered, his voice tense with anger. "I take it they enjoyed their stay?"

"They did – except for one minor inconvenience," Holmes replied. "When the temperature rose each day, the wind would pick up. Sand would blow everywhere. They had to forsake the beach and take their picnics *sur l'herbe*."

"How very interesting," our host replied, observing my friend carefully.

Holmes glanced my way. "Imagine Monet at his easel on the beach – painting with all that sand blowing about."

He glanced back at O'Clery. "We mustn't leave without once more congratulating the professor on the rigour and detail of this particular '*La Plage*'. It even replicates the hundreds of particles of sand the sea-breeze spattered over Monet's canvas while the paint was wet…I wonder if the copyist's accuracy of each particle's placement could be confirmed by the Deuxième Bureau in Paris?"

The professor's cheeks flushed. In an alarming *volte-face*, the brows had come down, almost touching each other, and the look had turned malevolent.

"For my amusement, Mr. Holmes," he snarled, "tell me about this Robert Miller's death. You say it wasn't an accident. What sparked your suspicion? Did this malefactor – whose preparations you say were at the level of genius – make a – "

" – serious blunder? Only the one," Holmes confirmed.

"Go on," O'Clery demanded.

"His choice of the four-in-hand – the American Quarter Horses. For power and speed from a standing start they are nonpareil, entirely suited to his devilish purpose, but I could find no other instance in the whole of the Queendom where they would be used to pull a cab."

Holmes turned and walked toward the door. I followed. "A last word," O'Clery called out as we opened it. "You praised the blackmailer regarding his preparations, and the forged Miller letter 'above all'. Wouldn't such a skilled practitioner of coercivism have a second, even third and fourth exact copy to hand? Food for thought, Mr. Holmes…"

The door shut behind us. The young seminarian who led us to the Professor's study caught sight of us from the quadrangle. He hurried over to escort us out. Conversationally, Holmes asked him, "How do you get on with the professor?"

"He's all right – as long as you stay on the good side of him," he replied, glancing towards O'Clery's rooms. With a wry smile he added, "But heaven help you if you rile him, as I did once. In an instant he turns into a chthonic Fury."

Back on the road, Holmes selected a lone barouche from a line of hansom cabs.

"That's the first I've heard about a Schumann concert this afternoon," I said. "A bit feeble as an excuse to get us out of there, wasn't it?"

"Not at all. You and I *are* going to the Hallé straight after we change our clothes. I ordered the tickets last night."

"Holmes, that terrifying eruption and the threats have convinced me O'Clery's our blackmailer. The explosion was triggered when you mentioned grains of sand. Can you explain? And why are we now going to a concert?"

Holmes chuckled. "I assume you noticed I drew my thumb across the painting the moment I had my back to O'Clery?"

"I did," I replied, "though I haven't the faintest idea why you should want to leave a thumb mark on it."

"Ever since I discovered my grandmother was the sister of Horace Vernet," Holmes began, "I have taken a special interest in French art. About ten years ago a Parisian gallery dealer by the name of Durand-Ruel became interested in the new exponents of Impressionism – Monet and Pissarro, for example. He was intrigued by their preoccupation with surface texture. He grew into a connoisseur, buying up their paintings by the dozen, adding works by Sisley and Degas and Manet. He organised a series of exhibitions which transformed the art world's former hostility into acceptance and admiration. It was evident to art dealer and crook alike that in time the paintings would shoot up in value, Renoirs and Monets not least. Six years ago, a criminal mastermind organised a break-in at the Durand-Ruel Gallery on the Rue

Laffitte. Hundreds of thousands of francs-worth of paintings were cut from their stretchers and spirited away, including '*La Plage de Trouville*'. All were returned for a ransom except the Trouville painting. Clearly it was a favourite of the mastermind behind the theft."

I gestured back towards the College. "But that was a copy. It can't be worth ten guineas. If it were the stolen Monet, the professor would hardly hang it in full sight over the mantelpiece in his study!"

Holmes replied, "You've heard the adage, if you want to hide something, do so in full sight. O'Clery knows that."

"You have yet to explain why you ran your thumb along the paint. If it wasn't to leave a print on it, why?"

"Some time ago, an acquaintance with the Deuxième Bureau's Paris headquarters contacted me. They knew Horace Vernet was my grand-uncle. They asked me to keep an eye open for the stolen Monet. Remember, it was never ransomed. The Bureau felt it might well have been hidden within France's borders for a year or two until the search went cold. Then it could have been smuggled abroad. They told me of a clue hidden in the paint, a clue which – if you can get close enough – would show it really was '*La Plage de Trouville*' rather than a good copy. Like other Impressionists, Monet layered dabs of pure colour on the canvas, sometimes wet on wet – you apply a new layer of oil paint on top of a still-wet layer, rather than waiting for one layer to dry before applying the next.

"A major feature of a coastal resort like Trouville is of course the beach. From the artist's point of view, a less desirable feature is the in-shore wind which sent my parents packing into the interior for their picnics. Monet was working on '*La Plage de Trouville*' when that wind came up and peppered the still-wet paint with grains of sand, hundreds of which became set in the paint as it dried.

"It's almost impossible to see the individual grains unless you're within two feet of the painting and know what you are looking for and where to look. Even then you may have to be near a window letting in bright clear sunlight, which the professor's jabot curtains certainly did not allow. When I ran my thumb across the painting I could *feel* the grit. Think how unlikely it is for someone making a copy to have a spoonful of Normandy sand to hand, to scatter on the canvas before the paint dried, placing every fleck at the exact locus as the grains on the original, yet managing to do so before the final layer of paint dried.

"Nevertheless, O'Clery apparently felt perfectly safe keeping the painting on the wall. Monet skilfully captured the exact colour of the beach. It was when I remarked how accurately the copyist had included particles of sand spattered by the sea-breeze over Monet's canvas, and I referred to the Deuxième Bureau, O'Clery realised the game was up. The painting is the genuine Monet and worth far more than he could ever legitimately have afforded. His ferocious reaction merely confirmed we had the proof we needed."

I sat back in my seat, staring out. The streets grew more familiar as we followed the signs towards Paddington.

"All right" I cried. "I give up! We're stuck in heavy traffic! Do you want O'Clery to make his get-away? In heaven's name, why did you choose a stately barouche and not an agile hansom? Even now he could be packing up to make good his escape. Why tell the driver to take us to our lodgings? Why are we to go on to the Hallé instead of driving furiously to the Yard to inform Lestrade?"

"My dear chap," Holmes replied calmly, "we are on our way to our lodgings and the concert for good reason. When I said the blackmailer possesses one of the finest brains of Europe, with all the powers of darkness at his back, I meant it. From the moment we took Perrin on, there was never a likelihood we would inform the Yard or the Deuxième Bureau of the blackmailer's identity, or even that we have discovered the genuine Monet."

"And never a likelihood we would take the matter to the authorities is due to – ?" I asked.

"We couldn't leave O'Clery's study and rush off to Scotland Yard – quite the reverse. We had to make it clear to him that was exactly what we were *not* going to do. Hence my purchase last night of tickets for the Norman-Neruda matinee. The letter purporting to be from Robert Miller was a fake, but utterly brilliant in preparation, right down to Miller's own vellum stationery, script, and execution. Even now, if it were to arrive at the Royal Chemistry Society, Perrin would have no answer to the danger it presents to him. The professor made it plain he has an entire barrage of equally convincing fake letters at the ready. He could as readily avenge his capture by sending one anonymously even from a cell at Pentonville Prison. Our only option was to force a *quid pro quo* on him – he would forego the Velasquez but keep the Monet, and never again hold the forged letter over Perrin's head. We in turn – "

"We in turn – " I interrupted with disbelief. "We in turn," I repeated, "would let him keep his freedom, even though you believe Robert Miller was murdered, presumably on O'Clery's orders?"

"The timing of Miller's death and choice of horses convinced me it was murder, yes, but a forensic impossibility to lay at the professor's door."

He leaned to one side to catch our driver's attention.

"Cabbie," he called out, "be a good chap, zig-zag a little now and then, and let us know if we're being followed. There's an extra guinea in it."

Holmes turned back to me. "I wouldn't be surprised to find the professor or an acolyte following us in a hansom right now, to be sure we're keeping to our side of the bargain."

That evening we reminisced over a fine meal prepared by Mrs. Hudson where a bird was the chief feature, washed down by the promised bottle of Hochheim's Königin Victoriaberg. The dessert of wine-marrow pudding followed, straight from Godey's *Lady's Book.* At the end of our meal, Holmes folded his napkin and sat back, staring into the fire.

"Watson, I do not say this lightly, a shiver went through me at the look in O'Clery's eye when I revealed our identity. I have never before felt so deeply we were in the presence of some vast potency, a power of evil."

The time limit imposed by the blackmailer came and went. Four days later, Mrs. Hudson's stately tread was heard on the stairs. She brought a sealed package for Holmes which he asked me to open. It contained a letter from William Perrin expressing the warmest gratitude for our services. Our client had received no further communication. The anonymous bid of six thousand guineas for the Velasquez had been withdrawn and the painting put into Christie's next auction of Old Masters.

The letter from Perrin was accompanied by an extremely generous cheque. It was time to set off for another celebratory dinner at Simpson's in the Strand.

The End

NOTES

Professor O'Clery. Not long after the encounter with Holmes and Watson the Machiavellian Professor disappeared, taking the Monet painting with him. He left behind not a trace of his former existence. It transpired he was to change his 'nom-de-guerre' from O'Clery to another Irish surname,

Moriarty, derived from 'descendant of Muircheartach', while still calling himself Professor. He covered his malign activities through scientific works, including 'The Dynamics of an Asteroid', a work lauded as ascending to such rarefied heights of pure mathematics there was no man in the scientific press capable of criticising it. He rapidly built a vast and subtle criminal organisation – until seeking revenge, on May 4 1891 he overreached. His path fatally met Sherlock Holmes's expertise in Bartitsu at a narrow ledge above the glistening coal-black rock of the Reichenbach Falls in the Swiss Alps.

Blackmail. For readers interested in an in-depth discussion on this legally very complex subject, I recommend the 300-or-so page Brooklyn Law School paper titled 'Competing Theories of Blackmail: An Empirical Research Critique of Criminal Law Theory' at http://ssrn.com/abstract=1477400

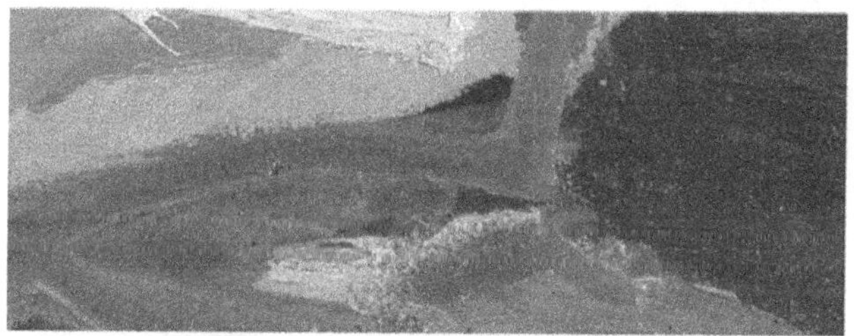

Sandy section from *The Beach at Trouville*

The Beach at Trouville by Claude Monet is in the collection of the National Gallery, London. It was painted during the weeks Monet spent at Trouville with his wife Camille and their son Jean. Camille and a female companion are shown in close-up, their figures apparently casually arranged and cropped by the picture frame, rather like a snapshot. Bright sunlight is conveyed in bold strokes of brilliant white, and

the women shade their faces with parasols. Grains of sand embedded in the paint reveal the canvas was painted at least in part on the spot.
Monet's earlier paintings of the Normandy coast had emphasised it as a working seascape, peopled with fishermen who had to contend with a cold climate, choppy seas and stormy skies. In this painting and the eight others made in the summer of 1870 he shows it as a holiday destination, with wide sandy beaches, bracing air and impressive seaside architecture.

Mauveine, or Florentine Mallow. While still a chemistry student 166 years ago, William Perkin discovered – by accident – the first synthetic organic dye in history, now variously known as aniline purple, mauveine, or Perkin's Mallow. After his discovery mauve garments were being worn everywhere, especially in London and Paris. Queen Victoria added to its popularity when she appeared at the Royal Exhibition of 1862 with a long gown dyed with Perkin's mauve. Perkins grew rich and famous. He continued intense research into dyes, inks and paints for the rest of his life, and perfected the manufacture of coumarin, one of the first synthetic perfumes, thanks to the so-called Perkin reaction.

'chthonic Fury.' Chthonic means 'of or relating to the underworld'. The Furies and the Eumenides were infernal female deities of vengeance in ancient Greek religion and mythology. The young seminarian clearly enjoyed displaying his knowledge of Classical Greece to visitors.

ACKNOWLEDGEMENTS

Dr Ian Dungavell, Friends of Highgate Cemetery Trust, both for his expert description of the famous Cemetery and for a suggestion he made which I incorporated in the story, namely 'Not sure if my colleague Nick got back to you, but we thought that one potential thing would be that a sketcher near there might be drawing the Beer Mausoleum, built 1876-78. Julius Beer himself died in 1880 and was interred there on 8 March 1880'.

Professor Alan Dronsfield who chairs the Royal Society of Chemistry's Historical Group. Especially see his paper on William Perkin's mauveine, 'An experiment that wouldn't work – and the discovery of the first synthetic dye' and the Brown, Cooksey and Dronsfield paper 'Perkin's mauveine – a fortuitous discovery'. Not for the first time, Professor Dronsfield solved my chemical questions. For a particular scene in my novel 'Sherlock Holmes and the Sword of Osman' he wrote 'yes, a lump of phosphorus will appear to glow in complete darkness, but the temperature must be kept low... It will inflame spontaneously at 30 deg C. To get the element on to clothing it would have to be dissolved in, say, carbon disulfide (itself a toxic, highly smelly and flammable solvent) and then painted on. And once the burning starts, it would go up like napalm.'
Stacey Smith, Visitor Information Coordinator, The National Gallery, who brought to my attention the sand particles in Monet's 'La Plage de Trouville', giving me exactly the story element I needed. She emailed, '...as Monet skilfully captured the exact colour of the sand, it is almost impossible to see it unless you are within two feet of the painting and knew what you are looking for (and where to look), and it was day where the room filled with bright clear sunlight. I can only personally recall the sand at the back of the chair being noticeable, but when I first saw it, I assumed it to be exposed canvas from where Monet had roughly applied paint, and I always found my eye drawn to the dark splotch on the back of the chair directly above the sand, leading me to forget about what I had seen.' With her colleagues at the

National Gallery she continued to answer my technical questions on the Impressionists' painting techniques, use of light en-plein-air, etc. Many thanks, Stacey and colleagues, much appreciated!

Andrew Jeskins, Programme Manager, Awards & Prizes, Royal Society of Chemistry, for information on which medals and prizes William Perrin in the story might have been in line to receive for his discovery of dyes from coal-tar derivatives, including two Royal Society of Chemistry prizes dating back to the second half of the 19th century: The Faraday Lectureship Prize (the RSC's oldest prize, first awarded in 1869), and The Longstaff Prize (first awarded in 1881), plus The Royal Society's Davy Medal (dating back to 1877).

Elizabeth Hunte, Business Information Specialist, The British Library, who emailed with information on William Henry Perkin and his patent. 'I ran a search using Blackwell Idealist, a historical DB datastore, for William Henry Perkin, there were 9 results. The 1st one is possibly what you are researching.' This was 'Perkin, William Henry'. Subject: Producing a new colouring matter for dyeing with a lilac or purple colour stuff of silk, cotton, wool, or other materials. Patent No. GB185601984A.

The Ambassadors' Skating Competition

It was a Monday morning and I was in my surgery. England's Capital lay under a lacklustre sky, the elegance of the Edwardian Era and *Art Nouveau*'s emphasis on greens, browns, yellows, and blues confined for the moment to the interiors of the great Town Houses of Mayfair and Belgravia. Discouraged by the unpromising weather, only two patients had so far drifted in. Pensively, I stared out at the London traffic. I had heard nothing of late from my former comrade-in-arms Sherlock Holmes, some three years into retirement on a bee-farm in the South Downs.

The Mansion House wall clock struck eleven. I sent my receptionist, Miss Campbell, off for medical supplies and reached for the day's *Times*. Militant Suffragettes had disrupted the State Opening of Parliament. An Anglo-Russian Convention relating to Persia, Afghanistan, and Tibet was about to be signed in St. Petersburg. Geologist Richard Oldham was proposing the Earth has a molten interior.

I decided to leave a note for Miss Campbell and go on foot for a meal at one of my clubs. The cream of the Clubland crop was located along St. James's Street. I would leave it to Fate which one I ended up in. Boodle's was enticing. It had been a while since I tasted their wonderful Orange Fool dessert. Then there was Brooks, and White's, the latter the most prominent of all, or on Pall Mall, the Army and Navy, and The Travellers – the latter's Pall Mall elevation inspired by Raphael's *Palazzo Pandolfini*. A principal qualification for membership was at least one journey of five-hundred miles from England. The Club was a haunt of several old Army friends from my time on the North-West Frontier with the 66th Berkshire Regiment of Foot. I glanced at my watch as I came to Pall Mall. The Travellers was nearest. I should be just in time for the excellent *déjeuner à la fourchette*.

I was wending my way expeditiously to the dining room when my attention was caught by a small group of men in the Billiards Room. They were deep in conversation, standing at the table with their cues raised like lances. "Why, it's the Sungazers!" I blurted out, my heart pounding. I recognised three of them immediately, first the German-born Sir Julius Wernher who through his activity in the Kimberley diamond market held the greatest financial power in the world. He was reputed to have the staggering personal fortune of some £12,000,000. Next to him was the Earl of Cromer, an Orientalist known for his belief in the 'White man's burden'. England's duty, he held, was to act *in loco parentis* to the less advanced peoples of the world.

The third was the famous 'Poet of Empire' and story-teller, David Siviter, with eye-glasses as thick as gig-lamps, who lived in a Jacobean iron-master's house deep in the Sussex countryside. Rumours abounded that Siviter was in the running for the Alfred Nobel Prize in Literature, in consideration of his remarkable talent for narration. The award would come with 138,000 Swedish Krona. A fourth person seemed hazily familiar. The fifth I had never seen before. "So the Sungazers and the Kipling League still live," I breathed.

There was a good reason for my pulse to race. Holmes had suffered one of the most humiliating defeats of his illustrious career at the hands of the mysterious Kipling League, a case I recorded against his will. The League at that time consisted of Siviter, Sir Julius Wernher, Sir Alfred Weit, and the Earl of Cromer. Holmes and I had dubbed them 'the Sungazers' because of their South African connections. The Sungazer is the heavily armoured dragon lizard *Cordylus giganteus*, the largest of the cordylids. It lives in underground burrows in the boulder fields and rocky outcrops of the high veldt of the northern Free-state and southern Transvaal – where the goldmines are. "I tell you, Watson," an angry Holmes had warned at the time, "notwithstanding that some deem them the greatest subjects of the Crown, no crook and loafer in all the underworlds of New York or London has the edge over them."

A billiard room steward came out of the stock room carrying boxes of *Romeo y Julieta* cigars. I reached out as though to engage him on the subject of cigars but instead said *sotto voce*, "Steward, I have a question. The gentlemen at the billiard-table…I recognise Evelyn Baring, now Earl of

Cromer, recently Britain's Consul-General in Egypt. The slight fellow next to him is the story-teller and poet David Siviter. On his right is the Randlord Sir Julius Wernher, but who are the other two? And do you have any idea what they're discussing so intently? They appear to have forgotten why they're standing at a billiard table."

The steward asked, 'And you are, sir?"

I told him.

"Did you say Dr. Watson, sir?" he exclaimed "*The* Dr. John Watson, Mr. Sherlock Holmes's biographer?"

I inclined my head in assent.

He stood for some seconds looking at me speculatively. "Even so, sir, what happens at The Travellers doesn't happen, if you know what I mean. I *did* overhear some of their conversation, but you know that my job would not be worth – "

" – a Lady Godiva?" I interrupted, using Cockney slang for a five-pound note. I reached toward my inside pocket.

The steward broke open the top box of cigars and held it out to me, whispering, "The man leaning on the table, the one with the round head – that's Sir Otto."

"Sir Otto who?" I whispered back, selecting a cigar and sniffing at it.

"Sir Otto Weit," came the reply. "You must remember his older brother, Sir Alfred, sir? A Randlord just like Sir Julius. Sir Alfred died last summer."

I held the cigar up as though to determine the price. Instead I asked, "And the other fellow at his elbow? There's something familiar about him."

"Lord Minto," came the reply. "Governor-General of India."

"Ah yes," I said. "He served with Lord Roberts in the Second Afghan War. He's a lot older now."

"You were in that war too, weren't you, sir?" the steward remarked. "I remember you saying so in one of your stories."

"I was," I nodded, "until we took on Ayub Khan west of Kandahar and a marksman got me with a ten-rupee Jezail. Ended my Army days."

The steward told me he too had been in the British Army. "Served in the Anglo-Zulu War, under Lord Chelmsford."

We were now on sympathetic terms. I bobbed my head towards the billiard room. "The subject of their conversation?" I murmured. "They look very conspiratorial."

The steward's hand came forward and took the five-pound note.

"Hardly, sir. Mr. Siviter was telling Sir Otto all about a lily-pond he plans to dig in his gardens in Sussex."

"A lily-pond?" I queried.

The steward nodded. "Yes, sir. He was explaining it in detail. Seems Sir Otto also plans to dig a lily-pond at his country estate. Lord Minto seemed very interested in ponds too, except not particularly for lilies. Something about his old days in Canada – ice-skating during their dreadful winters."

My dubious expression showed how little I felt I was getting for the five-pound note now in the steward's clenched hand. I would keep the cigar for my next dinner at Simpson's. The steward started to turn away. He stopped.

"There *was* something else, sir," he continued. "A Russian's name came up. That's when they went into a sort of huddle. Made it much harder for me to hear what they were saying."

"What about this Russian?" I asked.

"Well, sir, it seems they're going to invite him to Tewin Water."

"Tewin Water?"

"Sir Otto's country house. It's in the same part of the country as Sir Julius's estate, Luton Hoo, but even bigger."

He went on. "I'm trying to remember the Russian's name…Yes, it's beginning to come back, sir…" Expertly his hand took the second 'Lady Godiva'. "Now I remember – Count somebody or other. Something like Beckerdorf."

"Count Aleksander Konstantinovich Benckendorff?" I asked. "The Tsar's Ambassador to the Court of St. James?"

My companion snapped the cigar box shut.

"That must be the one, sir. Alexander was his first name, without a doubt. Same as my brother, Alex."

I had now missed the *déjeuner à la fourchette*. I walked on into the well-populated Outer Morning Room. I would bring the fact of the meeting to Sherlock Holmes's attention. With Alfred Weit dead, it seemed the mysterious League had recruited replacements in the form of Alfred's younger brother, known for his impetuosity, and Minto, both probable members of the British Empire League. Sir Otto was as fanatical in support of the British Empire as his older brother had been. Under the spell of Cecil Rhodes's imperialist vision, it was Otto who had encouraged the ill-fated Jameson Raid ten years earlier, attempting to annexe The Transvaal for Britain.

If this assembly of the richest and most powerful men in England was up to something, Holmes might be tempted to come out of retirement – not least to seek revenge. Forgive and forget was not a virtue readily associated with him. But why would such men meet in the sanctity of The Travellers' billiard room simply to discuss digging lily-ponds? Did inviting Count Benckendorff to Sir Otto's country house mean anything in particular? Why would anything to do with the Russian diplomat be of special interest or concern to the Sungazers?

On the walk back to Queen Anne Street, I stopped at a post office and scribbled a note to Holmes. A dismissive letter came by return.

Dear Watson,

As far as I understand, it is not yet considered unlawful assembly if a gaggle of extremely rich men meet in the billiard room of a London club. If something more substantial about the conclave comes across your path, let me know.

A fortnight went by. I was in my surgery after examining Lord ----- whose predilection for show girls had led to certain complications. The second postal delivery of the day dropped with a clatter inside the Tradesmen's entrance. A large square envelope with a Marylebone postal marking jutted out from among bills and circulars. I took it outside to a favourite bench under the branches of a London plane tree. It contained an ornate invitation card headed '*Winter Merry-Making at Tewin Water, Welwyn, Hertfordshire*', followed by -

Sir Otto Weit invites you to attend a Winter Festival champagne and beefsteak reception at his country estate to celebrate the inauguration of the Minto Skating Club. This will be followed by a tripartite ice-skating competition between the Ambassadors of France, Russia, and the United Kingdom. France and Russia will be represented on the ice by His Excellency Monsieur Paul Cambon and Count Aleksander Konstantinovich Benckendorff, the United Kingdom by Sir Arthur Nicolson, 1st Baron Carnock GCVO, Her Britannic Majesty's Ambassador to St. Petersburg. The prize will be awarded by the 4th Earl of Minto, whose skating expertise derives from six years as Governor General of Canada.

RSVP Lady Lilian

The date was '*to be set soon after the first heavy frosts of the winter*'. Guests would be informed suitably in advance. Neither my name nor any other of a guest-to-be had been inscribed. Instead, in large letters in lurid red, someone had scrawled *'It will have blood, they say. Blood will have blood.'*

I put the card away and set off for my afternoon constitutional. Despite the dramatic reference to blood, I was disinclined to bring the matter to Holmes's attention after his cool reaction to my sighting at The Travellers. Or ought I to tell him? He said if something more substantial came across my path I should let him know. This card had arrived only two weeks after spotting the Sungazers at The Travellers – surely no coincidence?

I entered the Regent's Park and settled on my favourite bench by the lake. I came to a conclusion. I would inform Holmes by telegraph but underplay it. '*Holmes, it may be of no interest whatsoever, and completely coincidental, but...*' I would quote word for word the two obscure hand-written sentences. I left the park and made my way to a nearby post office.

The next day brought an urgent knocking at the front door. I flicked a sixpence at the expectant telegraph messenger boy and took the small envelope. The wording was brief. I was to come down to Holmes's Sussex farmhouse at once. I was to bring the envelope, as well as the invitation card.

The motorised cab from Eastbourne Station rumbled into Holmes's yard and halted alongside the verandah. My old friend was waiting for me. Together we went into the sitting room where to judge by the warmth and the deep pile of glowing embers the housekeeper had laid the fire at dawn. Holmes held out a hand with an eager look.

"The card, please, Watson."

"'*It will have blood, they say. Blood will have blood'*," he read out, adding "'*Stones have been known to move, and trees to speak*'. It's Macbeth's Lament, Act 3, Scene iv."

"What do you make of it?" I asked.

"There's a saying 'The dead will have their revenge'. One death foreshadows more deaths to come. Whoever sent this is telling us there's a conspiracy to murder. He sent this card with the aim of thwarting the intrigue. I'm inclined to take up the challenge. We have the 'when and where'. A murder will take place in a few weeks' time at Sir Otto Weit's Estate, daringly in broad daylight, before a considerable throng to boot. We must visit the scene well beforehand. In case we are apprehended, we shall go equipped like men from the National Mapping Agency. Bring a camera and a book of mathematical tables. Repeat what the steward told you about the Sungazers' conversation in the billiard room."

"Not the most gripping exchange you'll ever have heard, Holmes," I replied apologetically. "Siviter was describing a lily-pond he plans to construct in his garden in Sussex. Mostly he was addressing Sir Otto. This skating competition indicates Sir Otto will by then have his own pond. Also, the Russian diplomat's name came up. The steward gathered enough to know they planned to invite the man to Sir Otto's country house."

"The Russian turns out to be the Count on the invitation card?"

"He does. Count Aleksander Konstantinovich Benckendorff."

"Now the envelope," Holmes ordered. He looked at the postal mark. "Marylebone," he muttered. "Remind me, who else was present in the billiard room?"

"Besides Siviter and Sir Otto, there were the Randlord Sir Julius Wernher, Lord Minto, and Evelyn Baring, 1st Earl of Cromer."

My companion crossed to a shelf and pulled down a copy of Debrett's *Peerage and Baronetage*. "Marylebone," he repeated to himself several times, flipping from name to name. "Belgrave Square, no." Then, "Bath Street…that's Piccadilly, not Marylebone." Finally there came "Ah, good! Wimpole Street is within the Metropolitan Borough of St. Marylebone."

"Hardly a five-minute stroll from my own premises," I confirmed. "Why do you ask?"

"Because the Earl of Cromer's townhouse is at Number 36, Wimpole Street. The lackey dispatched to post the card was too lazy even to stroll down to a post office in Mayfair. One last thing… in your Army days, in addition to your medical work, did you engage in such activities as military sketching and so on?"

"I did," I replied. "Attachments on the North-West Frontier required training in map reading and field sketching. I still have my old sketching board designed for use on horseback. It came with compass, inclinometer, ruler, a roll of paper, and an arm buckle."

"What constitutes a good field sketch?"

"It should show the north arrow, then the scale – how many inches to the mile. Ridges, valleys, saddles, isolated farmhouses or even villages. Why this sudden interest in my Army days?"

"Ponds too?" came the query.

"Yes. Sketching lakes and ponds too."

At King's Cross Station, I purchased a copy of *The Strand Magazine* to read on the journey to Welwyn and joined Holmes in a first-class carriage of our own. We reached our destination just after dusk. Under a half-moon, we emerged from a thick windbreak of Scots Pines on the edge of the Weit estate, looking across a small river at an attractive Neoclassical building set in formal gardens. Every room was ablaze with electric lighting. At our feet was a pond the size of a small lake. Three small poles, each carrying a national flag, had been placed at predetermined places at the far side from a small wooden jetty. The nearest to us displayed the vertical bands of blue, red, and white of the French Tri-colour. The next had the three equal horizontal fields of Imperial Russia – white on the top, blue in the middle and red on the bottom – and beyond it the Union flag, the red cross of Saint George edged in white, overlapping the Cross of St. Patrick, the two superimposed on the Saltire of Saint Andrew.

Holmes raised an arm. "The fresh pile of earth across there from digging the pond," he asked. "Does anything about it strike you as unusual?"

"Quite a lot of clay in it," I pointed out. "That's what you'd expect from any large excavation around the London Basin."

"I didn't mean its geology."

"Then what?"

"The sheer quantity of soil. It must have occasioned an awful amount of work on the part of farm labourers, yet even the largest waterlilies prefer a depth of no more than thirty inches."

It was time to start to work. I took a bearing on geodetic North with my old army compass and sketched in silence. Holmes stood by, preoccupied with the pile of excavated soil and the flags. Suddenly he asked, "You must have dealt with situations where someone topples into icy water – crossing foaming rivers on rope-bridges in the Afghan mountains in winter, perhaps? What's happens within the body?"

“Blood is immediately redirected from surface tissues to the brain, lungs, and not least the heart.”

Holmes responded, “I meant, what happens to the human who happens to be in the body at the time?”

“Perfectly straight forward,” I replied. “Cold shock can bring on cardiac arrest. Death quickly ensues.”

“How quickly?”

“Often within a minute.”

This was followed by silence. Then, “Those flags.” Holmes pointed. “The Russian flag – it’s placed between the other two. What do you make of that?”

I studied the positioning for a few seconds.

“What do I make of that?” I repeated. “Nothing.”

Holmes continued, “I presume the winner is the one who skates across the pond, retrieves his nation’s flag, and gets back to the finishing line before the others. Count Benckendorff is the only one required to skate across the very middle. Why are the flags so far apart? They could easily be clumped much closer together. Ambassadors are very likely to know which flag’s theirs.”

I returned, “If you want to me finish this sketch, Holmes, do keep any such inquisition for our journey home.”

The moment we took our seats on the train for London, Holmes commenced with “We shall need a few inconspicuous auxiliaries. Resourceful. Daring. About half your weight. Suggestions?”

“I’ve no idea what you’re up to,” I replied, “but you’re describing to perfection our old ragamuffin friends, the Baker Street Irregulars. They were daring and resourceful. As to weight, they never had a decent meal except when you employed them for a day or two. I doubt if even their leader Wiggins weighed more than seven stone.”

The street urchins in question were Holmes’s unofficial force during our Baker Street days. Holmes paid them a *per diem* of a shilling with a handsome bonus on providing a vital clue.

"Exactly who I had in mind!" Holmes exclaimed. "We'll see if Wiggins' successor, Simpson, is at the old haunts. Meanwhile, we'll make use of our old sitting room at 221B. We need waste no time in arranging the meeting."

After moving to Sussex, Holmes had purchased the lease of 221B, Baker Street from Mrs. Hudson, and he retained the property for those times when he needed a base in London. Two days later, and promptly at two o'clock, the street door received a hammering. Mrs. Hudson could be heard expostulating, her words drowned of any meaning by the clamour of high voices. A swift pitter-patter of naked feet was followed by a half-dozen ragged little street-Arabs rushing into the room. One of their number, taller and older than the others, gave a sharp order.

Despite the rough and tumble of their entry, they instantly drew up in line and stood with expectant faces. The leader stepped forward with an air of lounging superiority, disarming in such a disreputable little scarecrow. "At your service, Guv'nor," he said, a mock left-handed salute knocking his dark grey flat cap to one side.

"And your name is – ?" Holmes enquired.

"Nick, sir," came the response. "Wiggins and Simpson and that lot gave up the street, sir," he explained. "They've got themselves wives and proper jobs, bless 'em, sir." He waved a hand proudly at his companions. "We're the new Baker Street Irregulars, at your service, Guv'nor. That is," he added, looking hopefully from Holmes to me and back, "if there's money in it."

"There is," Holmes assured him. "We'll offer the old scale, a shilling a day each, one day's pay in advance. You'll get your orders now. Be ready to execute them the moment you hear there've been a few hard frosts in Hertfordshire.

Post one of the Irregulars at King's Cross railway station. Anyone arriving on a Great Northern train will know about the weather in Herts. Understood?"

"What about a bonus?" Nick pursued, taking the unusual commission in his stride. "I heard you gave a guinea each for anything 'ceptional."

"Guineas there will be," Holmes agreed. "Watson, give Nick here the sketch you made so they can find their way to the pond at Tewin Water. Now, Baker Street Irregulars, listen carefully…"

As we left the building my cheery smile to Mrs. Hudson turning to a frown. I confronted my friend. "Now look, Holmes," I expostulated, "I know you like to keep me in the dark until the very last moment, but surely I'm entitled to an explanation. For example, why did you give the Irregulars money to go to the ice-rink in Westminster and learn to skate?"

"My dear fellow," came the amused reply, "surely it shouldn't be left just to aristocrats and Ambassadors to enjoy recreation on frozen ponds?"

"That I can agree," I replied, "but why order Nick to purchase – or more likely steal – a supply of waterproof gloves and buckets? And why order his 'aide-de-camp' Fred to buy a six-foot pole – and why an auger? Where is he about to drill holes?"

"Ah, Fred and the length of bamboo and the auger. Yes, life does have its little mysteries. You must wait a while before you learn the reason for those."

"Holmes," I retorted, "I must warn you, nobody should confront such rich, powerful, and ruthless men head on. We learned that lesson a few years ago. We are not of their ilk. They'll ride rough-shod over us again. We don't have the tools their wealth provides. You have a fine reputation – the finest in fact – but as a *Consulting Detective*, not a Randlord whose worth exceeds that of many a state, or someone who has spent a life-time governing subcontinents like India, or countries like Egypt. Country squires and one long-forgotten French artist are numbered in your ancestry. You have had to make your way to considerable fame solely on your wits and deductive powers. By contrast, the Kipling League have pedigrees miles wide, and bank-balances miles deep. They not only know the system in which we guppies swim, they are the very ones who *created* the system."

I saw Holmes to his Sussex train. Back at my own premises, I propped the invitation card against the mirror on the hall table. I stared at it, arms akimbo. What was the sender up to? What was Holmes up to?

New Year's Day came and went. *The Times* reported the lowest daily temperatures on record across Britain. A communication (again anonymous) arrived, giving a date for the Tewin Water skating gala. I let Holmes know. The reply came.

Have instructed Irregulars to prepare for their mission. Beforehand, I want to play you a piece on the violin. Come down soonest."

"'Play you a piece on the violin'," I repeated aloud. The words generated a pang of nostalgia. On occasion during our Baker Street days, he would play a Mendelssohn's Lied on his Stradivarius. The age-hardened wood resonated wonderfully. By contrast, left to himself he would seldom produce any music or attempt a recognised air, instead he would throw the fiddle across his knee, close his eyes, and scrape away.

I made arrangements for a *locum* and took the morning train to the Sussex coast.

Holmes's housekeeper cleared away the lunch plates. The remains of the pork joint were earmarked for Tallulah, her much-loved prick-eared Norwich terrier. Holmes stood up. He gave the already-blazing fire a further poke before reaching for his violin. "Now," he explained, "I asked you down because I'm about to play you a piece from Mozart's *Magic Flute*. Note the position of my fingers..." He held the violin forward. "...and especially the note produced when I hold these two fingers down on the third string."

"Holmes," I protested, amused, "It's not my intention to take up the violin. I have enough on my plate treating my aristocratic male patients for syphilis or, if female, the bad effects of wearing tight corsets. Bedsides, my hearing has nowhere near the auditory quality of yours. It seems you have the heaven-sent gift of perfect pitch."

"Nevertheless," Holmes commanded, "do pay particular attention. There's a special reason for this little exercise. Tomorrow we shall be returning to Tewin Water."

Once more we emerged after dark from the thick line of Scots Pine on Sir Otto's estate. Temperatures across the country had remained freezing even by day, reflected in the pale layer of ice on the surface of the pond. Holmes placed a violin case against a tree. It contained a cheap instrument he had specially purchased for our mission. I kept an ear open. Rustling from behind us would announce the approach of Nick and the Baker Street Irregulars.

The half-dozen small figures appeared at our side like dragon's teeth rising from the damp soil. The troupe shook our hands in a surprisingly formal manner. In the starlight, the dark clothing Holmes had ordered for them combined with thick daubs from burnt corks across their foreheads and cheeks made it impossible to spot them against the scaly orange-brown barks of the wind-break behind us. The

Irregulars emanated an air of collective expectancy, staring at the pond and then beyond at the well-lit Regency house. Three had pails at their unshod feet. Two of them were struggling with a thick wooden plank. Their leader Nick held a claw hammer. The smallest two had skates dangling from their necks. One of the latter carried the auger and the length of bamboo.

"Like you asked, Mister 'Olmes," Nick said, pulling one of the skaters forward, "this'n's the musical one among us – not much more than four stone neither. Used to sing treble in a boys' choir until his mother and father got run over by the Great Northern coach. Dead on the spot."

With the Irregulars at our heels we retreated some hundred yards into the Scots Pines. Holmes opened his violin case and pointed the bow at the musical urchin. "Listen carefully," my friend ordered. "Memorise the highest notes."

The beautiful *Queen of the Night* aria filled the glade.

We returned cautiously to the woodland edge. The musical urchin strapped on the skates. With surprising facility the tiny creature glided away from us. His arms remained at his side until quite suddenly, nearing the middle of the pond, his right hand shot up. "Excellent!" Holmes exclaimed. "Watson, mark that spot on your sketch. He's telling us the ice is producing a High C."

"Holmes," I whispered, "I've gleaned from all the palaver with your violin that High C is important in all this, but what does it mean? What does it matter if the ice produces a note like Lilli Lehmann singing '*Casta Diva*'– or if it just rumbles?"

"Something I learned from the King of Scandinavia," Holmes whispered back. "Skating radiates a tone whose frequency depends on the thickness of the ice. A low rumble means the ice is thick, it can easily support your weight. The thinner the ice, the higher the tone. High C means the ice is barely three inches thick. Anyone even a stone heavier than our young friend would already have crashed through into the freezing water."

A few minutes later I passed the sketch-pad to Holmes. The area of the pond outlined by the skater whenever he raised his hand revealed an extraordinary fact. Through the middle of the pond there was a single stretch some twenty feet in length and six feet wide where the ice was dangerously thin.

"Why," I asked, "would the water freeze in that particular pattern? Surely – "

"Left to Nature it wouldn't," came the reply. "The Sungazers have arranged it so." His bony forefinger tapped at the pad. "They must have covered this patch with matting of some sort while the rest of the pond was hosed with water, ensuring the ice on the outer areas grew thick enough for a grown man's safety. It means they've earmarked just the one skater for an unpleasant death. You look doubtful, Watson. Well, with young Fred's help, you shall have your proof.'

On Holmes's nod, Fred picked up the auger and the bamboo and eased his way on to the frozen pond. He began to drill a succession of holes, plunging the cane through each, raising an arm whenever it failed to touch the bottom. Almost exactly under the patch of thin ice lay a trench more than eight feet deep, extending in a straight line towards the flag of Imperial Russia.

"As I thought," Holmes said. "How else could you explain the sheer quantity of earth over there? The only skater obliged to cross the very middle of the pond – precisely where the ice is thinnest – is the Russian Ambassador. Weighed down by skates and winter clothing, his veins charged with champagne, the Count will plunge into freezing water right where the pond is deepest and where rescue within several minutes the least likely. Except," he added, "the mighty Kipling League, for all their miles-wide pedigrees and miles-deep bank-balances, will now be thwarted by Nick and the Irregulars. If the Kipling League are bent on murder, it is our obligation to prevent it. If it was Cromer who forewarned you, he has achieved his aim – the survival of the Russian Ambassador – even if for reasons we cannot divine."

Taking his cue to commence, Nick broke open a hole in the thicker ice 'off-piste' with the claw hammer just large enough for the buckets to draw water. Rhythmically the tatterdemalions took turns sending already near-freezing water swirling across the patch of ice overlaying the trench, thickening it with each inundation. At last, after satisfying ourselves we had left no clues to our presence, we returned en masse to the railway station where Holmes saw the motley crew into a third-class compartment and paid them with a "Well done, Irregulars!" and the gold guinea promised to each.

On the day following the festival at Tewin Water, I went through *The Times* with a tooth comb. A short report on the event said a fine time had been had by all. The Russian Ambassador had won the skating competition.

A week later a most curious incident occurred at my surgery. At dusk the receptionist saw the last patient to the front door and went home herself. Within seconds a sharp rap came at the Tradesmen's entrance. I walked past the hall stand where the card still lay and opened the door to find a most unexpected visitor, Sir Julius Wernher. He said, "Dr. Watson, as Francis Bacon tells us, '*If the mountain will not come to Muhammad, then Muhammad must go to the mountain*'. May I come in?"

He pre-empted my acceptance by stepping past me. I pointed to the consulting room. The Randlord settled himself on the settee while I took a comfortable chair and looked at him with some apprehension.

"I should mention that my doctors give me less than five years to live," he began. "Nevertheless, I'm not here on medical matters. It cannot go on, Doctor, it really can't. There must be a truce between the Kipling League and you and Sherlock Holmes."

An expression of incredulity must have passed over my face because he quickly continued. "If not friendship, then understanding. If not understanding, I really don't know what to say without sounding menacing, which is not my present intention by any means. Three or four years ago we were challenged by your friend Holmes over the matter of a corpse found in a pond at Scotney Castle and we came out on top. Hands down. This recent matter at Tewin Water had a reverse outcome. In both instances, our goal was of the utmost significance to England and her Empire.

"At Tewin Water, our aim was to prevent the proposed Anglo-Russian Convention from coming into being later this year, a pact which aims to overturn centuries of enmity between St. Petersburg and London. Sir Edward Grey and Count Benckendorff have just announced it'll be signed in a few months' time.

"When you and Holmes prevented us from removing the Count from the negotiations, it meant we will fail in that aim. By our own failure, we failed the British Empire. Despite the blandishments of the Tsar's foreign minister Izvolsky we believe the Convention will act as a fig leaf to mask continued Russian activities against England's interests in Persia and Afghanistan. Worse, St. Petersburg will continue to make every effort to wrest control of your immense trade with British India, the Jewel in England's Crown, the fabulous land which supplies your traders with pepper, raw cotton, silks, porcelain, fine spices, tea, and coffee – and gains you your world prestige. Lord Curzon said as long as England rules India, she remains the greatest

Power in the world. Lose her and you drop straight-away to a third-rate Power."

I remained silent. I had no idea how to respond to his words. Then, as though from nowhere, he asked, "Doctor, I believe you were at the Battle of Maiwand? You will know Siviter penned some verses to the men who fell there?"

At once the opening lines came back to me.

There was thirty dead an' wounded on the ground we wouldn't keep –
No, there wasn't more than twenty when the front began to go;
But, Christ! along the line o' flight they cut us up like sheep,
An' that was all we gained by doing so.
I 'eard the knives be'ind me, but I dursn't face my man,
Nor I don't know where I went to, 'cause I didn't 'alt to see,
Till I 'eard a beggar squealin' out for quarter as 'e ran,
An' I thought I knew the voice an' – it was me!

Yes, I reflected. That was Siviter, poet of Empire. I could hardly bear to recall the poem, so deeply did I pine our losses in the face of Ayub Khan's unstoppable onslaught. In vivid dreams, I would still see the graves dug so hastily of the soldiers we left behind on that lonely plain – even wish myself interred with them in the dusty ground.

My visitor continued, "Do you remember how great were your losses?"

"The 66th was worst hit," I replied. "We lost sixty-two percent of our strength."

"What did that mean in numbers of men," he pursued remorselessly, "Grenadiers, Indian troops, and so on?"

"Nine-hundred-forty-eight soldiers, and twenty-one officers dead."

My forehead furrowed. “Sir Julius,” I went on, “I don’t wish to be impolite, but your presence here disturbs me. If it isn’t for medical reasons, please explain why you’ve come to my surgery. It’s hard to believe it’s to reminisce about a defeat so tragic for my Regiment and for me personally.”

“On the contrary,” came the reply, “that *is* why I’m here, Doctor. Do me the kindness to respond to one or two more questions on the men who paid so dearly. Wouldn’t you agree those Tommies’ lives were utterly wasted? Didn’t you leave the majority of their corpses to rot in the dust, the flesh open to predation by wild dogs while your Regiment fled?”

I felt my face reddening with anger.

“Look here,” I retorted, pointing towards the hallway, “you may retrieve your hat and gloves, sir, and leave. Those men were among the bravest and most patriotic – ”

My words came to an abrupt halt. My uninvited guest made no move to leave. Instead he was nodding sympathetically.

“Indeed,” he said. “They stood and died because the British Empire called on them to do their duty, am I correct?”

“You are,” I replied, mollified.

“And they responded magnificently,” Sir Julius continued. “Without their willingness to die for the British Empire, your country’s influence in the East might have come to an end. Every officer and every Tommy Atkins knew if you were pushed back, the Great Game between the Russian Empire and British Empire might be lost. Tell me, Doctor, which other Power might wish to rival you for hegemony of the Indian subcontinent, keen to undermine your control of much of the Black Sea and Persia?”

“Still only the one,” I returned. “The Russian Bear.”

Sir Julius got to his feet. “Thank you for your courtesy in receiving me,” he said, bowing slightly. “As I expected, on certain aspects of Weltpolitik we are in complete agreement. I hope I have given you my reason for being here this evening. I wanted to express my admiration – yes, as a German – for the British Empire. It safety is the Kipling League's primary motivation, in fact its very *raison d'etre*. Above all others across the span of human time, your Empire conducts itself with majesty, a force for good in a benighted world. It fosters peace and prosperity, innovations in medical care, education and railways – civilisation itself.

"By contrast," he continued, "behind the mask of friendship, behind the Janus mask, Russia remains a predator, the Russian Bear sitting on the tail of the Persian cat while the British Lion looks on. She will continue to eye Persia and British India like the hot-eyed wolf eyes the lamb. Those of us in the Kipling League shudder at the very idea of an Anglo-Russian Convention. It will not halt Russian expansion – it will encourage it. In Central Asia, it will hinder rather than further the quest for security for your overland routes to the East. As to Tibet and Korea – the Kipling League sees no reason to trust Petersburg one *diuim*."

We left the Consulting Room and moved towards the Tradesmen's entrance. The Randlord stood at the hall table for a moment, pulling on a pair of fine leather gloves. I was uncertain whether to offer him my hand.

"Dr. Watson," he continued, "we have agreed the British Empire is a magnificent civilising force, its physical integrity in need of protection at all cost. Tewin Water was meant to be the *pièce de résistance*. You lost nearly a thousand men at Maiwand. We would have accomplished far more with the death of just one slippery diplomat, Count Benckendorff. If you had let the Count fall through the ice, the Convention might have been postponed *sine die*."

"Sir Julius, before you go – the ingenious plot?" I asked. "Who came up with it?"

"I did," came the reply. "On the 15th of January exactly forty years ago, the ice cover on the boating lake in the Regent's Park collapsed. Over two hundred people plunged into the lake. Forty died in the freezing water."

"One last question," I added, pointing back to the invitation card on the hall table. "What reminded the Kipling League of my and Holmes's existence?"

"We Germans have the word *Ansatz*," Sir Julius answered. "It means 'educated guess'. Siviter recognised you at The Travellers, speaking to the Billiard room steward. A five-pound note plus the threat to have his job taken from him convinced the fellow to relate the conversation. Nevertheless, your involvement in the Ambassadors' skating competition came as an unwelcome surprise."

A gloved hand rose, pointing behind me at the hallway stand.

"As to the League…the card which brought you and Mr. Holmes in... I recognise Evelyn Cromer's hand. I should have had my suspicions. Imperial Russia is the foremost debtor country in Europe. Cromer's brother, Lord Revelstoke of the Baring Brothers and Company, is leading secret negotiations with St. Petersburg on a very large loan by an international syndicate of bankers. The proposed terms are £50,000,000 at 89.25, commission 3.875. Barings wouldn't want that wrecked. At all costs he would want Count Aleksander Konstantinovich Benckendorff to be with the Tsar's foreign minister Izvolsky and your Sir Edward Grey to ensure the Anglo-Russian Convention was signed. I should have known Evelyn wouldn't be with us on this one."

With that he was gone.

The End

NOTES

Holmes's Stradivarius violin. One of the more unlikely claims made by the author Arthur Conan Doyle is that Sherlock Holmes purchased his Stradivarius, which was worth at least 500 guineas (Sterling £525), for 45 shillings (Sterling £2.25) at a pawnbroker's shop on London's Tottenham Court Road. Can anyone point me towards that pawnbroker? I'd like to see if he has any more Strads.

David Siviter. *'Poet of Empire' and story-teller, David Siviter, with eye-glasses as thick as gig-lamps, who lived in a Jacobean iron-master's house deep in the Sussex countryside.'*

Readers will realise from my description he is loosely based on the real 'Poet of Empire', Rudyard Kipling.

A Lady Godiva - a Five Pound note. Both Watson and Holmes can be very generous tipping someone for useful information. A five-pound note in the Edwardian era would now be equivalent to around Sterling £150, a tremendous emolument for a Club steward.

Randlord. Capitalists who controlled the diamond and gold mining industries in South Africa in its pioneer phase from the 1870s up to World War I.

The Randlord Sir Julius Wernher's worth of Sterling £12,000,000 in present value would be equivalent to Sterling £150 billion now.

Nobel Prize. In 1910 the award in monetary terms was 138,000 Swedish Krona. In 2021 it was 10,000,000 SEK, not far short of 1 million Sterling.

Orange Fool dessert. Professor Judith Rowbotham tells me an Orange Fool with similarities to the famous Boodle's

Fool can be made as follows: 'Take some oranges, grate off the zest, squeeze the oranges (and add some lemon zest for tang and also some juice because that helps to 'set' the cream), add slightly warmed sugar (about a couple of ounces to each orange). When the sugar has dissolved, pour the mix in a slow stream into already-whipped cream and keep "beating the heck out of said cream" until the orange syrup is mixed in. Pile into a bowl with sponge fingers and leave until the cream sets. Decorate - fresh oranges, angelica slices etc - send to table and wait for the applause. And like Boodle's famous Fool, clearly it must be eaten with a silver dessert spoon!'

Mendelssohn's Lied. Mendelssohn's song, for example 'Lied Ohne Worte', i.e. Song without words. This title for the pianoforte pieces is more closely associated with Mendelssohn's name than any other of his compositions.

Four Stone. "Like you asked, Mister 'Olmes," Nick said, pulling one of the skaters forward, "this'n's the musical one among us – not much more than four stone neither." A stone is a unit of weight equal to 14 pounds avoirdupois (just over 6 kilograms), and still used, in varying degrees in everyday life in the United Kingdom, Canada, New Zealand, Australia, and some former British colonies, despite their official adoption of the metric system.

Weltpolitik. The foreign policy adopted by the Kaiser Wilhelm II of Germany in 1891, marking a decisive break with former '*Realpolitik*'. The aim was to transform Germany into a global power through aggressive diplomacy, the acquisition of overseas colonies, and the development of a large navy.

Geodetic North. Watson is an expert on the use of compasses from his British Army days in India. In case you are interested, a geodetic survey determines the precise position of permanent points on the earth's surface, taking into account the shape, size and curvature of the earth. Geodetic North is also known as True North or geographic North.

Janus mask. In ancient Roman religion and myth, Janus is the god of beginnings, gates, transitions, time, duality, doorways, passages, frames, and endings. Usually depicted as having two faces.

Diuim. Russian measurement: 1 inch or 2.54 cm.

The Kipling League. Holmes's and Watson's first encounter with the powerful but secretive Kipling League came in *Sherlock Holmes and the Dead Boer at Scotney Castle* (2016, MX Publishing) by Tim Symonds, now into the 2nd Edition.

SHERLOCK HOLMES
AND THE
DEAD BOER
AT SCOTNEY CASTLE
2nd
EDITION
TIM SYMONDS

www.ingramcontent.com/pod-product-compliance
Lightning Source LLC
Chambersburg PA
CBHW070616310726
48982CB00001B/95

* 9 7 8 1 8 0 4 2 4 2 9 0 2 *